THE COCK'S EGG

THE COCK'S EGG

ROSEMARY NIXON

NeWest

A very special thank you to Aritha van Herk, Bob Nixon, Nicole Markotic, and Steve Smith for their suggestions, encouragement, and editorial advice.

I offer my appreciation to Eric, Merle, and Craig MacKenzie, and to Dr. Betty Bridgeman for their support both in Zaire and in Canada.

Thank you to David and Carol Roth for the generous offer of their cabin to finish my manuscript.

I gratefully acknowledge the Alberta Foundation for the Literary Arts and the Canada Council for financial assistance during the tenure of this project.

A number of works influenced and informed parts of the narrative. *Chameleons Dragons in the Trees* by James Martin; *Household Stories by the Brothers Grimm, 1886; English for Africa* by David Mills, Boniface Zodeougan, and Tim Doust; *Zaire Perception and Perspective* by Robert E. Smith and Diawaku Dia Nseyila; *La Maladie et La Guérison* by Kimpianga Mahaniah; and *A Book of Good Poems* in which I found Vachel Lindsay's poem, "The Congo."

FROM THE INSIDE OUT

Freida counts off what happened the first five weeks.

One. Her tampons blew up. In this humidity their bodies mushroomed, spread, until they popped the confines of their pink plastic shells.

Two. The legal rep came to their house to say Freida's sewing class for village women would start within the week. He implied embroidery, handstitched blankets, knitted baby vests.

"I don't sew," Freida said. "I don't know how to sew."

Three. Linford translated recipes into Kikongo for their cook. So now Freida cannot recognize the language of her food.

> All Kinds Vegetable
> *Nge tula manteke na nzungu*
> *2 mbala kuzenga*
> *1 kopo mosi de mbizi*

Mbizi? Where would they get *mbizi?*

Four. She discovered rabbits copulating. That fighting, scrambling in the cage, the female's enraged eyes. When the male mounted, her head half turned in disbelief. He hung for an instant, held the light, and then his sharp squeal, his topple as if felled. It made Freida look at Linford with new eyes. The mother died, they sold the buck, and now it's Freida's job to feed the babies. She carries lettuce, oatmeal, a small handful of peanuts out to the rabbit hutch. Bends to scoop twigs from the kerosene cans that encase the hutch's legs.

"Willie! Mademoiselle! Blanche!" Already they're falling over one another in their haste to sniff her fingers. She picks up Mademoiselle. Linford discovered she is male, but the name suits. The first few weeks Freida fed them milk from a medicine dropper, their shaking bodies cradled in her hand. Now she carries them daily to the house, lets them skid and frolic on the cement floor, leave their little turds behind her curtains.

"Ko-Ko." A boy of maybe thirteen stands on her doorstep. He's holding a dead animal — bristly and dead. Freida calls "Oui?" from the shade and the boy jumps and grins. She sets Mademoiselle gently onto the wire hutch floor, and the boy pushes behind her through the torn screen door to hand a smeared note. *I come from take the lesson Anglish supplementary at you if you not busy in afternoon.*

"Je regrette. Je ne donne pas de leçons supplementaires."

Ngafia, the school surveillante, the only woman who speaks to Freida on this compound, says the village women pity her. No baby, Ngafia says. All alone in this big house. I teach to you Kikongo. You want teach English lessons? Ngafia says. Maybe cooking? People sorry for you, you got no life but feeding rabbits. Infamous Freida: the village women avert their eyes, the men shift when she walks in front of Linford in her blue jeans, instead of two steps behind. Or when she calls, "Bonjour, Citoyen," before the men acknowledge her.

The boy is offering the bristling animal in both his hands, his body bent to her. Freida's never seen such a creature before. Often, sitting in the heat of the house waiting for Linford, Freida lets her mind go blank. Now it blanks of its own accord.

The boy makes a slight pushing motion with his hands.

"Qu'est-ce que c'est?" she asks, and near the roadway running past her house a man bends over, laughing. The boy thrusts out the animal again. Is this a gift? A dare? The thing looks like a cross between a porcupine and a pig. Unequivocally dead.

"Qu'est-ce que c'est?" and inexplicably the boy cradles the animal back against his thin shirt, freeing two hands to reach out in supplication. Is he asking for his note? Freida places the smudged paper in his palms. With both her hands. She's learned that much Zairian culture. The boy gives a small dejected bow and slaps down her path in his barefeet, the prickly dead animal upside down, staring.

▚◭▚◭◾

Two o'clock. Heat leaks through the air vents above the windows, washes the hot plate in gray-yellow light, hangs above the smooth cement. Freida lies on the bed and pages through her Purity cookbook from Calgary. Stuffed Pork Tenderloin Garnished with Apple Rings. Veal Marsala. Oyster Scallop. She and Linford saw meat at the market once. Something indistinguishable. Hard and hairy. Meat here is masculine. French Riviera Torte. Cold Praline Soufflé. Peach Melba. But mostly she craves cheesecake.

"Why do they call it cheesecake?" Linford says. "There's no cheese in it."

"There's cream cheese."

"That's not cheese."

In Calgary, Freida went to book club meetings once a month. She bowled. But here she feels a hollow in her chest that caves her in. She lacks gravity, may slowly spin off into some other orbit. Her shape is shifting. And she's been bleeding for a month. She pulls the bedroom curtain closed and changes pads. The smell. The rash. Tampons would have held this in.

Freida wanders through the living room, past the fireplace that stinks of bat pee. Zairians cook outside, and in this heat what expatriate would light a fire? But Linford wants the place clean, rid of junk. Her blown-up tampons, two years worth, are in large plastic sacks against the outdoor fireplace, along with several hundred pantry cockroaches overdosed on Baygon, waterstained papers, a boot, an earring, two broken desk drawers, a torn board game of Sorry. Freida feels junk suits this place, alive with insects, lizards, snakes, cockroaches. Why prune a garden in the jungle? But Linford aspires to order.

"If you find yourself with nothing to do, why not scrub out the cupboards?"

"If you finish up your work (what work?), you could always plant a garden."

Freida digs matches from Linford's toolcase and heads out to the yard; the smell of manioc is toxic in the air. Her fire smoulders. She pokes with a large stick, stuffs papers tight against the back wall; a burst of flame. Freida watches the hazy fire through the hazy heat until the road beyond their house and the steepled brick church in the distance ripple, undulate, as if breathing on their own. Linford will be pleased she took initiative. She'll document this in her diary. Today I burned trash.

Sometimes Linford stays the night in Sona Bata or Matadi, giving seminars or selling hoes. He takes his precious vegetable seed, carefully spooned and sealed into small plastic packages. Each package labelled. According to Linford, people walk for days to hear him lecture on "The Successful Introduction and Evaluation of Improved Manioc Strains." Freida pictures the produce — yard long beans, gardens of onion and Chinese cabbage. Linford collects metal from car wrecks and produces charcoal burners, rat traps, axes, hoes. Blood seeps between her legs. Maybe she should take a taxi now to IME compound. See a doctor. She's never bled like this before. Linford says it's nerves.

"What. Nerves make a person's uterus drop out?" she asked him. Linford only noticed because *he* plans to have a child. His motives write themselves across their silence: A baby would give her focus in Zaire. This baby cannot imagine itself into Freida's existence. A miniature Linford. What would it do? Make gagging noises to indicate she should pick up its toys? Hold its breath until she wiped up its spilled milk?

"Tampons blow up here," she told Linford. "Imagine what happens to babies."

"What is the matter with you?" Linford asked, each word edged.

That night she baked a cake, an orange cake with fresh orange juice. Linford stuck his thumb in the batter and extended it under her nose.

"What's this smell like?"

"I don't know. Cake?"

"Rabbit."

He wiped his thumb on the dishrag and Freida saw Frazer Sanway, a mean boy from her childhood whose left thumb ended at the knuckle. He used to insert it in his nostril to make girls gag. Linford sat down at the far end of the table and sighed over his peanut sheller blueprint. Freida washed out the dishrag and went to bed.

Ngafia sees Freida at her fire and heads over from the girls' dorm with a potion to help Freida conceive. When you give birth, "drop the baby," she says in halting French, you feel his body slip between your legs. "Un moment incroyable."

"I don't want a baby," Freida says, and Ngafia stares at her, unblinking, through orange flame.

The flames turn to smoke. Freida jumps to find a charred lump of something emerge from the fireplace. The lump veers towards her, pulsing. It looks like a blackened piece of the Whole Roast Pig With An Apple In Its Mouth that they ate for

Christmas dinner with the American oilmen she met at AERWA. Real potatoes. Liquor, not *malafu*. Freida danced with a lot of men. Each time she looked at Linford, he was eating. By New Year's he had reached 183. For dessert: Chocolate Marbled Cheesecake. One of the oilmen dancing with his hands on Freida's shoulders, said, "These are beautiful." In Zaire she can always bare her shoulders. Even nights, she rarely needs a sweater. "A little butterfly," he said.

Freida lifts her arms to catch the ash that floats like heavenly blessings. That song she used to sing, hands floating air. "The rains came down and the prayers went up, And the house on the rock stood FIRM," and she'd smash fist against palm. Decisive child. Linford knows where he stands. Linford wants the trash cleared. He wants a baby. Freida stepped on the scales the day after Christmas dinner. Ninety-three pounds. She's less now. She can feel it. Her shape is shifting; she's less definitive.

The burnt thing shudders. Pulses. Hops. Only now does Freida recognize the body of a large toad beneath the charred and crusted skin. He drags, hops, shivers, drags again. Stupid. Couldn't he recognize a fireplace? Couldn't he feel the heat? Freida reaches for her stick and wallops. The body makes a popping sound, smears the cement. A slip of charred skin flutters gently into air and Freida feels her weightless body drawn up with it, past hazy palm trees, while below her, hot air breathes around her body's imprint.

The fire burns itself out and Freida scrapes up the toad remains without a second look, drags the charred boot and ashes across the compound to the garbage pit.

When Freida heads out to the hutch to change the rabbits' water, she sees the red-striped single engine Cessna come and go at IME compound; so she'll be alone the night. Probably Linford's been invited to preach at the village meeting, he's delighted when asked, imagines himself a preacher, he takes tracts everywhere. Or perhaps there's been a death. Then he'll catch a ride to Kimpese in a truck tomorrow. He gets sick on small planes, especially Dudley's, though he won't admit this. When she and Linford flew to Vanga for a week, (Freida would fly daily if she could — the sudden rush of take off, the upward tilt forcing her line of vision above the palm trees to puffs of highbanked cloud, that drawing upward upward into blue), Linford discreetly vomited at the Bulungu landing.

Dudley, who emergency-landed near Kikongo last July, made crash-landing jokes en route.

"Is that Kikongo below?" Linford said gazing downwards to a clump of pointed roofs, and Dudley sang out, "Yep!" Beneath them another world, miles of savannah, clumps of brilliant green. Ten minutes later the plane banked over a small dotting of huts.

"Or, no, hmm, no, or is *that* Kikongo?" Dudley said. "Oh hell, we'll just fly until we get on course or run out of gas."

Freida laughed. Linford pursed his lips, his skin grey-green, and blinked down at his hands as if surprised by the sight of fingernails. Even in the sky, Linford needs his geographic boundaries. Maps have stationary places on them. Marriages have children in them. When they landed, the cockpit rushing hot with air, villagers lined the bumpy grass runway as if the three of them were celebrities; Freida could believe this. Children tore through the lifting dust, turned cartwheels, yipped and chased the plane as Dudley circled and bumped to a standstill by a mud brick hangar.

"A touch of malaria," Linford said and wiped his mouth.

While Dudley refueled, children raced in close-cut circles, dusty legs skidding.

"Hi-eee," "Eeeat," *"Mundele,"* they shouted. "Cheese." One

boy sang in high falsetto "Strawngers een the neet," and daringly brushed Freida's skirt with flicking fingers.

"Bebé? Bebé?" the children called to Freida, and the women grinned and stared and moved their childbearing hips to a soundless beat. The wind blew hot and moist, flipped Freida's skirt about her legs. When she climbed back into the plane, rejuvenated, Linford was already strapped into his seat, complaining of the large Zairian woman who pushed him, elbows jabbing, in her haste to climb aboard.

"Survival of the fittest," Dudley said.

Linford handed Dudley a map he'd sketched of the villages between Bulungu and Vanga.

"That right?" Fingers already whitening around his knees, his lips compressed, his baleful stare. Prepared for take off.

※◆▽◆▽◆※

Three-thirty. Freida walks down to the Source to bathe. Her face and body hot and sweaty, her hair and sundress reek of smoke. Above her swirls a flock of butterflies, a rooster, head cocked, beak open, running speedily beneath their flight. A village woman and child overtake Freida as she climbs down the hill.

"*Mundeli,* donne-moi du savon," the woman says.

"I have no extra soap for you. C'est impoli, ça," Freida tells her. The child stares at Freida's elbows. The woman answers nothing.

At the Source, Freida makes her way to the small enclosure she has claimed as hers. She lays her towel out on a low bush, spreads her shampoo, her soap, slides off her dress and panties, and slips into cool brown water. She scrubs her body to rid it of smoke smell, sinks below the surface. A water snake glides by at eye level, sleek and green.

The house is silent, reassuring, on her return. Only a trace of animal smell lingers. She washes her hands in the kitchen sink and sets beans and *saka-saka* on the hot plate. She'll read romances in bed until she falls asleep.

▨◭▧◆▧◭▨

Freida dreams that she is giving birth. But the baby springs from her head. Bits and pieces of baby squeeze sharply from her skull, an elbow, an ear, a buttock stinging, stinging — will the child never be released? The infant's prickly body pokes needles through her eye. Listen. Listen. She wakes to slapping. She is slapping her head, slaps at the stinging baby who is whimpering, while around them ashes fall. Lying in the muddle of hot sheets, she opens her eyes to blackness, turns to Linford's hot form; he's not there. Ouch! Ouch! Something's living in her hair. She jolts up, closes fingers near her scalp and squishes. Crusty wetness. Listen. Plop. Plop. Intense stinging on her breasts, her stomach. She crouches in the bed, crying, ripping away the sheets. Army ants plink about her, scurry up her in the blackness and when she finds the flashlight, she sees her bed a red-black tussling nest. They fall from the ceiling in a gentle shower. They grow around her. A clutch of them scramble round the indent of her knee. Where's the Baygon? Where is Linford? Linford's in Sona Bata, afraid of falling.

▨◭▧◆▧◭▨

In the morning's hot light, Freida carries the lettuce and oatmeal dish back from the rabbit cage, sets it gently on the cupboard, sweeps up dead ants, dumps live ants from the sugar bowl's shining rim, and crushes them beneath her sandal. She is so wide awake her head feels cocked, like a weapon, when in truth she hardly slept.

"You don't fight army ants," Linford will say. "You let them move through. You know that. Freida! You fought them with a little can of Baygon? You fought them with kerosene?" She will not tell him how she raged and gasped for breath, how she could not let that rippling wall of insects infiltrate her house, eat out her sugar, her pineapple, her yams, the beans left on the cupboard. She will not let Linford know she shouted them down, living room wall an undulating mass of red-black bodies, sweat burning in her eyes, how she lost herself in the small heady power, spraying Baygon, pouring kerosene in corners, disrupting their perfect drill formation, her feet firm on the floor, her body giant, occupying its rightful space. His face will turn duteous, righteous, his voice will rise up out of him so calm. "I thought you knew better. Just clear out and let army ants move through. Don't fight a battle you can't win. Oh, Freida!" And he will sigh. She hears him surely as she sees the rabbit hutch.

The rabbit hutch is bright in sunlight. The house smells of kerosene. By the tap at the far end of the path, a small girl washes her crying brother in cold water. The teacher Kavula is putting up a bamboo fence. Freida's skin itches with angry bites, dead ants cling to her hair. She should walk to the Source and wash again. The wind's picked up. Wind without rain, that doesn't usually happen. Her eyes so dry. She holds her body firm and weighted, allows no shudder underneath her ribs.

"Put the legs of the rabbit hutch in cans of kerosene," Linford said back in September. "Then army ants, if they come through, can't reach the rabbits." He grunted as he raised one corner. Freida dragged a can beneath its leg, and Linford lowered the leg into the liquid. "Ants eat the eyes out first, and then the insides, especially in babies." He lifted the back end and Freida slid a second slopping can of kerosene.

After the broom and dustpan are put away, Freida washes the cool floor with bleach. The smell mixes with the kerosene and dust. She realizes suddenly her bleeding's stopped. She carries the bedding to the garbage pit, shakes dead ants down. They tumble, trickle, turn in jerky rhythm. She gathers her skirt away from her and shakes. Dead palm fronds swing brittle in the rising heat.

When she is ready, Freida pours a glass of lime juice and carries it with her. The rabbit hutch is close to the back door. Freida walks the length of the porch, steps down among the fern and weed. She drinks. The liquid spreads a pattern of cold gossamer through her chest. Only then does she kneel in the bare, firm dirt beside the rabbit hutch, and twine her fingers in the sticky filaments of spiders' webs that bridge the lip of the kerosene can to the hutch's leg. She stays crouched so, cheek pressed to the rough wooden surface, sunlight thick in her throat, till her ears fill with the faint drummm of a truck motor toiling up the grade.

Then Freida lifts the three flat rabbit bodies by the legs, and lays them in the garbage pit. She feels the need to wish for something, but can think only of cheesecake.

When the truck grinds to a halt on the compound, Freida is a long way off, scrubbing herself in brown water, erasing ants from her hair.

TRAPPINGS

Quelqu'un?" Annie bolts upright in bed. A rustling. Silence. Scrape of insects against the window screen. Don't move. Movement is foolhardy. Suspect. The window open, the night black.

"Est-ce qu'il y a quelqu'un?"

A scrambling from the attic floor. A rush. A pounding.

"Au secours!"

Lie back. It's only rats. Didn't the Vanga missionaries warn her? Rats in the ceiling. They can't get down. She listens. A palm nut rolls across the floor, followed by a herd of scampering feet. Zairian football. They slide, the front ones skid into the wall.

"Touchdown," Annie says and, sinking to her pillow, turns to sleep.

Annie spends the morning painting in the hall. A hole in the ceiling knocked out of the plasterboard, a vent hole, moves air through the hall down to the bedrooms. Couldn't someone have cut it out neatly? A wire mesh spreads itself across the hole. A breeze rises upward. Lifts the skirt of her gold-flowered sundress. She must be careful not to dabble it with blue. Annie looks up to see a large rat lying spread-eagled on the mesh, watching her paint.

Annie crouches in the grains of lemon-coloured light and cleans her paintbrush on the concrete patio. The muscles in her arm are tight and tired. She's erased dirty walls with thinned-down colour; stains disappear in the slow wash of heat. The beauty of the pale blue paint, the spattered flecks, constricts her throat. Milundu exudes a smell unto itself: the thick texture of *fufu*, September's lethargy; a citrus-tasting village, bittersweet. And now these Zairian scents mingle with her own: paint thinner, sweat, Arrid Extra Dry.

Yesterday she cleared the back bedroom — dragged out old motors, rusty tin cans, termite-chewed boards. An American, single, male, lived in this house for three years. Then it sat empty. So far cockroaches seem scarce. But there are sand fleas. And the rats. Annie dips a hand in her drinking barrel. The water brown. She'll boil it. Last night she took her first bath in the stream. A tributary of the Kwilu. It takes skill to grasp soap in moving water. "Oh for soap on a rope!" she sang. Only the forest birds answered. "La Seine a de la chance," she recited to a screeching parrot, a bit of poetry coming to her from French lessons in Belgium. "Elle n'a pas de soucis. Elle se la coule douce. Le jour comme la nuit." That's what Annie's going to do here in Africa. Leave her worries behind. Belong only to herself. Annie doesn't need another bath. She needs to take the path behind her house into the forest. She wants this strange new road, Zaire, to carry her. She looks down at her blue-streaked arms. Deserts her paint tray. Sets off.

Late afternoon light stains into green above the silt road. Behind her, deep throaty voices sing, then fade, somewhere — in the church?

O mono ngizidi ya samba; Inga, inga

The air cools as she leaves Milundu behind.

O Vingila yakubama
Vingila yakubama
Inga, Inga

Annie passes through citrus trees and comes suddenly upon a farm. The area is barren of grass; a boy of maybe fourteen sits on a fallen log, fashioning a flute.

"Bonjour, mademoiselle."

The building behind him is a fragile hut of sticks plastered with mud. This and the other farm dwellings are flanked by pistachio-coloured greenery and palm. A slender young woman the colour of burnt sugar steps from the hut. Her hair is plaited in a dozen braids. She wears a shirt of virgin white. And blue jeans. The jeans fit tight and firm. No line of underpants around her thigh. Malachite earrings dangle from her ears, good malachite, not the rough stone Annie finds at market. Her body is not hilly like the teachers' wives with their many children. The boy, wearing a washed-out T-shirt and Fortrel pants, jumps to his feet.

"Je t'apporterai une poisson," he says, "car tu vois ma sœur." Then he turns abruptly to his work. Annie shakes her head, resolves to improve her ear for Zairian French. Perhaps fish-giving is a gesture of welcome in Zaire. Annie continues on the scabbed road leading past the farm, grasses worn bare. When she is almost out of sight, the boy calls, "Ma sœur aura une lettre pour l'Amérique. Pourriez-vous l'envoyer, s'il vous plaît?" Annie looks back to see a trace of white against the hut. Then it is gone.

"Bien sûr." Sure. She'll mail the young woman's letter. She heads into a valley. The boy and his sister sink from view over the crest.

Annie lights the coal oil lamp. In the clearing, egrets land in a small flutter. White and distant. Today Zairian children hauled her junk away. Today a child ran by on the forest path, guiding a metal barrel rim, a toy, steered with a beating stick. Today the blue-jeaned woman veiled herself in trees behind Annie's back yard and watched Annie pick mangos. When Annie called to her, she dissolved into the forest.

Annie should keep a diary. She should write home. No, Annie has not written to Canada; words locate her. She doesn't want this curious world invaded. Nor will it lock within the confines of her pen.

The school préfet, Citoyen Kididi, comes to her patio in the early evening to see if she has needs. No, rien du tout. Behind him, dusk splinters into twilight, softens the dusty palms, the ironwoods, the colocassia blooming yellow before her door.

Wide awake with optimism, Annie leans at her bedroom window, resting cool against the sill. The wind whispering from the forest's edge breathes her a melody, a woman's voice, high and plaintive:

Kalekanga ko, yo fuku yovo mwini

Annie strains, but sees nothing save the dark outline of trees. She slips beneath the covers.

O meto mawonso ketalanga

The voice cloaks her into sleep.

Six o'clock. A rapping at the back door. The boy. Did she not ask his name? Ngonzi, he says. Same brown Fortrel. He hands her a slimy whiskered catfish.

Freed of the fish, he wipes his hands on his pants, digs in a pocket and brings out a rumpled letter which he offers Annie between his palms. No stamp. He ignores Antoine, Annie's worker, who emerges from the forest. A polite nod to Annie, the boy slips away, followed by a bobbing, pecking rooster.

Antoine works in the kitchen, muttering, baking bread, preparing *mbika,* squeezing lemon, sprinkling *pili-pili,* roasting Ngonzi's fish on the hot coals. "Come and ee-eat," he calls, the only English he speaks.

The letter sits against the sugar bowl. Mr. Tony Lauber. Hesston, Kansas.

"Who is this Ngonzi?" Annie asks. Antoine's head jerks at the name. He grins anxiously, shakes his head, watches Annie, avoids touching the letter. He slaps his bread dough on the counter. "Mademoiselle, sa sœur. . . . Il y avait une chanson dans la forêt hier soir. . . ." His shoulders shudder as he kneads the dough.

"This woman," Annie waves the letter, "the boy's sister. Antoine?"

"Eiiii, Makita!" Antoine whispers, and sprinkles too much *pili-pili* on the fish.

▚◆▟▚◆▟◣

"Who is this woman?" Annie asks the Citoyen Kididi. Tonight his family's at her house for dinner, at her new home which smells of guinea fowl and whitewash.

You are satisfied? the préfet asked of his watered-down paint.

You alone get paint in Milundu, the Vanga missionaries

said. Your life is privileged. Zairians accept that.

The citoyen ordered Mama Kididi from the house once when the baby cried. At Annie's insistence, Kiampuku, the oldest, ran into the night and dragged her back. Mama speaks neither French nor English, sits frozen on her chair, eyes lowered, a wide statue chipped from stone. Does she wear panties? Kinshasa women spread their legs under their *nleles* and pee in the streets. They have discussed the rains, the citoyen and Annie, the school, national holidays, the price of cloth, and now, "The woman and her brother, behind the compound, on the farm," Annie urges.

"Ah, Makita." The citoyen frowns and his wife's eyes, startled, skim his face, then Annie's.

Kididi's three small daughters crouch at the table. The silverware, each dish, sets them on edge. They stare at Annie; their eyes flick to their father who wields a knife and fork in Western fashion. When Ebenga's slight fingers descend to her ball of rice, a sharp *"Sala ti luto!"* sends them flying for her fork in a spray of white kernels; she awkwardly raises the fork to her mouth, soft grains flutter through the prongs. Her sisters giggle, Mama shuffles the baby, and Citoyen Kididi frowns.

The Kididi family has made it through the Guinea Fowl *Mwamba,* the rice, the yams, the fresh tomatoes, the cornmeal biscuits. The *Mwamba* was spicy hot, but the girls peppered red their meat with *pili-pili,* their cornmeal biscuits, even their tomatoes — enough to blow off Annie's head — and still their eyes don't tear.

"Already someone has told you stories. Yes. Makita." He says softly to himself, "Some heard her singing last night in the forest."

Mama will not look at Annie. She wears a dark *nlele,* no earrings. Her stomach rounds up through the cloth as if a fifth Kididi is on the way. The citoyen stretches his legs under the table, his thonged dark feet, that muscular body, white pants, blue checkered shirt, open to the throat. Annie watches him play the part of Western ease before his family.

"Makita," he shakes his head. "Fragile as frangipani." Frangipani, the doctor's wife told Annie, when she asked the name of the delicate copper flower on the wide-leafed plant behind her door. A temple tree of fragrance and beauty. Centuries before the white man brought this tree to Africa, she said, Aztec Indians a continent away used the flower as religious rite offerings; whoever touched or smelled the flower after the rites was put to death.

"Ah, Makita. She was not wise."

Mama stares into her baby's wide blank eyes.

"Will she be my student?"

A muscle jumps in the citoyen's neck. "Mademoiselle, you do not understand. To even speak of her. . . . One year ago she was expelled from school. But we will turn to other matters."

Annie fetches the pies. "She does like blue jeans."

The citoyen eyes Annie strangely.

"Who spoke of her to you? The missionaries, I suppose. All that is finished. Citoyenne Makita lives in a world — how do you say? — of dream."

Annie spent several hours on these pies. Orange cream (oranges picked from her orange tree) and lemon meringue. Even with Blue Band margarine her crust flakes. Annie serves each one in turn, the citoyen, his wife, the three small daughters. The citoyen bends to his plate. Insects zing the screen. Full moon tonight. Annie can make out fruit bats swinging in the trees. Kididi takes one mouthful; his fork suspends. The three daughters scrape their filling to the side, and halfheartedly munch the crust. Eyes on her plate, Mama chews in quick, tight motions.

"But could I tutor her? Will you have more of anything?"

The préfet makes what Annie perceives to be a retching

motion into his hand. He pulls out a hanky, rubs his face, his nose. He stares morosely at his pie, says, No, ce n'est pas possible.

⬛◆⬜◆⬜◆⬛

Late afternoon Annie slips into the forest. Palms dapple the forest path. Palms soak her skin. She has no way of gauging how far she is into the trees, only the smell, a touch more thick, fruit sweetly rotting. Still. The forest holds its breath. And Annie holds hers. Green, like velvet. Annie throws back her head and watches butterflies flutter the leaves; squints, and they change to floating bands of blue and white and yellow, leave smoking trails behind their flight. Annie opens her eyes. The young woman in blue jeans stands before her, a load of firewood on her head. Her braids shine, coiled and fine, in the hot light. A tremor zips Annie like a lightning bolt. For a moment she's swinging, somewhere, out between the woman's body and her own.

The young woman lowers her bundle of sticks beneath a frangipani tree. She smells of earth, sunwarmed and pure. Thick sand swallows her bare feet.

"You are Makita?" Annie feels strangely out of breath. The young woman watches. "I mailed your letter."

"To America." The way Makita says America makes it sound exotic, and consummate in a way Zaire never could. Her shy smile leaps out of her like words.

A small dusty boy in torn shorts herds three cows past on the path. His gaze catches them, he shouts "Aya!" eyes large and frightened, and switches his cows into a lumbering run. The bovine smell hangs in the heat. The frangipani sways.

Makita rips a branch from the frangipani tree. Where it tears, the tree weeps milk. The orangy copper flowers crushed in her hands exude a sweet perfume. She drops her blossoms.

"Makita. Will you come to my house for tea next Saturday?"

But she is gone. Not disappearing slowly into the dark undergrowth, not fading to a dot along the trail. The singing grasses simply swallow her.

"Makita!" Annie calls. Only a forest bird answers, raucous, and she feels the sting of sand fleas on her arms.

▰◭▰◆▰◭▰

Sunday afternoon. Annie is invited water skiing with the Vanga missionaries. Water skiing? Yes, the construction manager for the new hospital has a motor boat and two imported skis. She walks the seven dusty kilometres which do not lead past the farm. Even so, she keeps a lookout for Makita and her brother who do not materialize.

> Tu es là

she sings

> O cœur de ma vie
>
> Et c'est toi qui me fait vivre

Annie climbs the last steep dusty hill that winds to Vanga village, and overlooks the Kwilu. Already she can hear the putt and roar of Pete Ragalski's motor boat. When she reaches the crest, the boat is screaming past the palm-lined shore that's packed with bobbing men, women, and children in parrot-coloured shirts and *nleles*. The crowd cheers, waves palm fronds at the water-skier, Pete's wife, Shirley, who has disappeared in a white-out spray. In the midst of this cacophony, Annie finds her American neighbours who have come down from their houses and gathered on the shore.

"Annie!" they call. "How are you coping in Milundu? Have you gone mad with isolation yet? It's been weeks. You must visit more often. How was dinner with the préfet?"

Annie tells them of her cream pies.

"Cream fillings are Western food, Annie. You're in Africa. Zairian's hate the texture. Orange cream! Reminds them of dung."

"Maybe they'd eat it as penitence!" The women laugh.

"So how's the house? The mess cleaned up yet?"

"That Tony. He sure was no housekeeper."

"You can tell by its state how organized he was," the women say to one another.

The doctor's wife pulls Annie into the shelter of her arm which smells of stale talcum and says, "Annie. We're glad it's you, not Tony in that house. That man ate enough uninvited dinners at my place."

The women sniff and say, "He did at all our places."

The boat has turned, Pete speeds by, relaxed at the throttle.

"Yes," says the doctor's wife, "but you didn't have a daughter to protect. He chased anything in skirts."

"Did he chase Makita?"

The women fall silent. Their faces sharpen. They turn their backs on Annie and watch the skiing. The doctor's wife sighs, says, "No, Tony liked white girls."

"Oh," Annie says. "Just the préfet said Makita was unwise."

The doctor's wife lowers her voice. "The préfet! He has his nerve . . . let me tell you, Annie, he's made it harder for us here to spread the Gospel. No, Makita was just another black girl dreaming of America."

Shirley, spread-legged, is heading west, chopping the waves.

"Tony. He used to arrive at my house at supper time, cling like a dung beetle, you couldn't get him out. And then he'd never help to clear the dishes. Why, once. . . ."

"But Tony knew Makita?"

"He paid her no attention, really. She was in his sixth form class." The doctor's wife grimaces. "Though the more girls Tony had mooning over him the better he liked it." She looks sharply at Annie. "The Citoyen Kididi. He caused the problem. Men! You mark my words. He'll be sleeping with a new school-girl this fall. No thought to his own wife."

It is the children who first grab palm fronds and tie them with wild grasses to their feet. Arms extended, they ski with drunken abandon down the bank, through the grasses, the coeur de boeuf, mow down the Rose of Sharon, to the river's edge. Their mothers, shrieking, fit palm fronds on their feet and hurl themselves behind their children.

"These people can be so infantile," the doctor's wife says.

"You know the rules yet, Annie?" The women have drifted back, bored with the skiing. "Don't allow students to your house for English help. Préfet's orders. Of course when Tony lived in your house the rule made sense! The citoyen will drag the student to the football field and shave her head."

Pete does a loop at the hippo pool and is revving back now.

"It's not uncommon punishment here, Annie, you learn to stomach things. He shaves their heads and leaves them kneeling in the sun. That's what happened to Makita, the whole school looking on."

"Those beautiful braids."

"Oh, those girls are used to it," the doctor's wife says. "But Makita, she left her brother — his name is Ngonzi, a sweet boy really no more than fourteen — and went away in shame. You won't teach him. He has no fee money for school."

The villagers climb and ski the bank, shouting in the passion of the moment.

"Of course, weeks later," the doctor's wife clucks and nods, "when they found Makita's body eaten out by insects. . . ."

Annie's own breathing fills her head. The crowd roars far away.

The doctor's wife wipes a handkerchief across her sweating brow in a dismissive gesture. "Anyway," she says to Annie, "I've had enough of this heat." Then adds low in Annie's ear, "The problem is the Zairians. A woman not two months ago went mad, jumped in the hippo pool and drowned. Swore she saw Makita on the forest road, smiling and beckoning her. They say Makita's trying to trap a soul, trying to reach Tony. Annie?"

At the head of the rocky path glide two figures silhouetted against the doctor's house. Ngonzi in Fortrel pants, and Makita, in a gold-flowered sundress. Flecked with blue.

The motor dies, followed by the slapping backwash of the Kwilu's current. For an instant there is nothing but the soft suck of feet in sand, and empty silence.

It isn't until late October that she places the rat trap under the roof. And early November before Annie, the dizzy scent of Zaire on her skin, hears in hot darkness the sound of a rat, lured by South African cheese, galumping back and forth across the ceiling, dragging the rusted trap by its broken legs.

CON/COCTION

This cock has slashing eyes. A crooked floppy comb. This blood-red cock. His acts stuck in your throat. He smells, if you ever get that close, of red dust and stagnant water. Tossed in, a spurt of *pili-pili*.

Crouched now in the shade, hottest part of the day, his feathers ruffled. Wind and white clouds sailing. Behind the refectory. Behind the church. *Cock with hens on a Zairian afternoon*. It could be a painting. His harem encircling. Notice his battle scars? His beak's broken. He's quiet. But he's not resting. He's watching. This one's a fighting cock.

A woman descends the mountainside, head piled with firewood. A basket of *biteke-teke* hangs on her arm. The path runs two kilometres to the east, spreads into a road, winds down among tall grasses and the occasional thorn tree. A still day in late September. The woman's feet stir dust and scurry army ants and dung beetles along the path. Her body rhymes with the

THE COCK'S EGG

sway of passing thorn tree branches. Passion fruit flowers hang bedraggled, dark-centred, like an old woman's hair. The woman steps over a tree, knocked down, uprooted, felled but growing. She reaches a village, passes huts, stands before her own. Unloads her firewood. Her husband lies on a hemp hammock. He is impotent. A spell cast by an angry prostitute he never paid. The woman hears voices. Smells cooking fires. Kneels. Scrapes away dirt. Lights her own fire. Boils a pot of water. Breathes in the evening air. Earth. Fire. Water. *Ke mbote ko,* her husband says, peering in the basket. He does not long for *biteketeke.* When he strikes her, all sounds of evening echo in her ears.

I had to tell my househelp: You go home when I say you can go home. It's not up to you to decide when the work is done. When I dismiss you, you can leave. Sometimes I think it's hopeless. How do you teach an old Zairian our value structure?

A Zairian teacher's wife invites herself to the *mundele* teacher's house for tea. Hot March afternoon. She admires the *mundele's* sundress. She spoons lots of sugar in the milky liquid.

You have such luck, madame, she says, despite the fact you have no children. In this we all pray God will bless you. You have a husband who speaks with you at dinner. You have a husband with whom to take a walk. Your husband never strikes you. My husband, he would like to live like your husband, but we have a reputation to uphold. Sometimes before we go to sleep, if I have made my husband happy, he pleasures me with stories of the way he could treat me. If he chose.

The woman sighs, wipes the nose of her smallest child on her *nlele,* sips her sugared tea.

I have a student, Nyadi, who used to push himself on me. He lived in the States for two years while his father studied. He switches to flawless English when I speak to him in French. The other boys don't like him. He puts on airs. Thinks he's too good for his sleeping quarters in the dormitory. Sits at the back of my classroom, quiet, doesn't work much, looks at me with those all-knowing eyes while I falter along in French. I sense he longs to be my friend, share his isolation here with someone who knows he knows another world. I'm polite, but I don't encourage him. How can I have him over? That's showing favouritism. Really, he has a North American attitude problem. He won't play football with the other boys, just walks around the compound all alone. Strange for a Zairian. Sure it's sad, but can I solve the problems of Zaire?

Two Zairian high school boys sit in June's cool evening on the *mundele* teacher's patio, reading pictures in American magazines.

Monsieur, one boy says, might I keep this for me? The boy holds in his hands a laughing grandma and grandpa on a porch swing. The elderly couple holds hands, looks into each other's face. The grandma's legs swing forward in delight.

I long for such a wife when I grow old, the student says. A wife American. If only she would be content to do the work.

The old man invites the missionary to his forest hut. They sit outdoors together on a fallen log. The man is barefoot and his shorts are torn. He speaks to his grandson. The grandson shimmies up a tree, picks a giant pod hanging off a vine. He hands the pod to his grandfather who bows and hands it to the missionary. The old man speaks. His grandson translates. Split this pod open. Inside you'll find a large seed-studded porous sponge. Shake out the seeds. Let the sponge dry. It will massage a tired back, scrub cooking pots, scrape callouses off heels. The pod is a parasite. But even a parasite can be put to use.

Sure I'd like to pay our househelp more. But if we start that, where will the taking end? Give a Christmas bonus, but not too big, or he'll expect handouts. If you pay your househelp more than sixty zaires a month, our househelp will envy yours. Ours will get surly. They may cast spells. It's important the *mundeles* keep a united front. Don't chat with your househelp. The more you listen, the more he will fabricate hard-luck stories of a sick child, an ailing wife. And watch your sugar. Always watch your sugar. It can take a new *mundele* months to clue in on how fast the sugar disappears. Barter down the statue vendeurs. For the sake of respect. Don't pay more than three zaires for yams. Don't lend your bicycle. Don't hand out pens. Once you have been here a while these guidelines will make sense. Think of it as the food chain. Allow the natural order to get out of whack, disaster results.

◄◊►◊◄◊►

This cock inside his scruffy maze of feathers spreads rumours, performs magic acts. That change of sex. That need for sex/ual apparatus. Blesses himself with dust, calls on the spirits. Pleasures himself. He has, after all, a harem to maintain. A cock can't be a cock without a harem.

This cock loves to run the road to Vampa Falls. Sometimes he heads out early, often a Sunday morning when his harem's lazing against the cool brick of the church. You might see him start across the football field, stride through the tall grass, sprinting now, neck stretched. Sometimes he detours on an insect chase. His head stuck in a bush, gorging himself on tasty moths. Hiding those eyes, bright, intelligent. But he never detours far. He watches. Vampa Falls can sense his coming. He pauses at her embankment. Buck buck bugocks.

So the Goddess caused a deep sleep to fall upon the woman earth and while she slept, the Goddess drew a deep rift in the earth. Where the woman cracked open, the Goddess pulled a rib and from the rib of woman, Goddess formed a man.

The cock is in awe of Vampa Falls. He knows she knows who laid the first egg. He's eaten from the mango tree. The truth makes him afraid. This cock. This con. His con/cocted stories are the only power he wields. All illusion. He steps into those feathers, takes another form. He tricks even himself, believes his hens would cease to exist without him.

Off he speeds, heading back. Flat cunning eyes. This cock misses his harem. A cock can't be a cock without a harem. His brown-red tail feathers patterned in light. He's tough, he's beautiful, this lying cock. He skims the foot bridge, cackles through the underbrush, across the football field. Skids against the dark light of the church. A cock and his harem. The hens, disturbed, cluck at his burden of pretension. Always the ache of knowledge, like an arthritic joint.

Some day a great she-wind will gather on Zaire's horizon. She will sweep savannah, blast village compounds, swirl the Kwilu's stream, rush up the Bangu. The great she-wind will lift the cock, those startled eyes. Will lift him light as dust, and carry him, ancient history, receding into distance. Till he becomes a pinpoint. Till Zaire cannot see him for the light.

PREPARATIONS

Y|ou know something about catching shrimp?" the girl says. "Me, I catch the shrimp I want." She lifts her skirt as if to curtsy, swings it left to right.

Gordie watches the girl, dressed in a blue and white school uniform. Maybe fifteen. Her short hair clings to her scalp like all the girls' hair at Milundu school. The préfet has strict rules, Ndadia says. Will not allow the girls to grow their hair and waste study time fashioning elaborate braids.

"Eiii, Ndadia," the girl says. "You did not attend church this morning. The Citoyen Panza is angry. You will lose points in your school cahier." Ndadia snuffs. The girl looks at Gordie and laughs.

Ndadia says, "Let's fish, Gordie," and he and Gordie shed their clothes and sink to their chests in sweet cool mud. The girl too slips off her skirt. She wears nothing beneath. She turns to hang her blue skirt in the palm tree and Gordie sees her buttocks, wide and happy. The mud down the riverbank squishes.

"Eiii." The girl sinks to her chin. When she comes up her body hangs thick with mud. They all three, giggling, rub their bodies in its thickness, dig tunnels that begin to close the instant they are dug. The girl wades to the mud's edge, squats, and deftly draws up three small fish which she tosses in Gordie's pail. Then Ndadia squats and works, earnest, in happy silence. Gordie joins them syphoning for fish and the odd shrimp.

"Enough," Ndadia says at length, looking at the sun.

"Come near, *mundele,*" the girl says. Her legs are longer than Gordie's, and wider. Ndadia splashes into the river and drops to a swim. Ndadia is brave to swim alone. He believes a *nkita* lives in the water. It can steal your powers. The girl puts out her hand and touches Gordie's mud-crusted underarm. Her hand travels down his side. They move into the palm trees' shade. The girl writes "Canada" across his chest and "groundnut" down his thigh. "Monsieur Lauber is my English teacher," she announces proudly. And slips both hands between his legs.

***

Gordie races through an overhang of trees and enters the sudden clearing of Lusekele village. The compound smells of lemons and mangoes and burnt goat hair. Ndadia squats before his house, chopping manioc with his coupe-coupe.

"*Mbote,* Ndadia."

Ndadia looks up, nods. A strip of hair has been shaved off the left side of his head. The Kunda family's monkey screeches, skitters up a tree.

"*Mbote,* Gordie."

"Caught speaking Kituba at school again?"

Ndadia shrugs.

Tata bends over the cooking fire in the courtyard, stirring a red-brown mess of eucalyptus leaves and bark and roots. *Coscos* for Mama's cough.

Gordie's Mom and Dad have tried persuading Tata to hospitalize Mama at the Vanga mission. The doctors at Vanga village say she has Slims Disease. But Tata spends days cooking *coscos,* and nights in the cemetery, calling on the ancestors for help. Ndadia's small sister stands over a termite hole, grabbing termites as they fly out, ripping their wings off and popping the insects in her mouth. The monkey chatters from the baobab, turns silent, scratches his behind.

Gordie ducks inside the smoke-filled interior of the hut and hands Mama a bag of coffee beans between his palms. Tata and Mama grin widest for South African coffee and Gordie sneaks whatever his mom won't miss — sugar, a few eggs, a sardine can — each time he visits. Once he brought cheese, but Ndadia said they fed it to the chickens. Mama's never been in bed at noon before. Always in the fields, coughing, leaning on her hoe. Right now she should be preparing *fufu, saka-saka,* and sardines for Sunday dinner. Her face, puckered like avocado skin, crinkles into smile.

"Gordie. Merci *mingi.*" She strokes his fourteen-year-old hand with her gnarled one, her finger curling and recurling as when a person beckons. Above her head, a small green lizard slips down the wall and plops behind the bed.

Tata Kunda clucks behind them, dips his head, and offers Mama the reddish mess of herbs and leaves. Mama smiles and shakes her head.

"Mawa mingi. She cannot eat. A spell's on her."

Gordie looks at Mama, her thin face folding in on itself. Insects sizzle in the lazy heat. She has a big sore on her jaw.

"Gordie! Hopscotch," Ndadia calls.

Five years ago, when they were only nine, when Gordie first moved to Milundu, he taught Ndadia hopscotch, and still Ndadia wants to play. By the time Gordie steps back outdoors into parched heat and startling sunshine, Ndadia has drawn the hopscotch pattern in the dust under the mango tree and waits, leaning on his stick.

"Kiadi. Mama is worse," Gordie says.

"She has pains in her stomach now," Ndadia says. He lands, spread-legged, throws hard his second stone.

Gordie says nothing, dusts his knees where he rests beneath the mango tree. Inside the hut Mama coughs, a hollow wracking sound. The monkey coughs once, loudly, from his tree. When Gordie looks up, the monkey is looking down at him warily, one hand cradled in the other.

"Last night Tata called Mama's clan together," Ndadia says. His voice is low and Gordie leaves the mango's shade to crouch beside him.

"They stood round Mama's bed. Tata said, 'Simbi, leave my wife alone so she can recover her health.' "

A rooster with a broken beak pecks dully in the dirt.

"But the witch doctor says perhaps her sister Simbi's not the cause. Now we must pay another goat. Tata blessed Mama and jumped in the air three times. Everybody spit in a bowl of water and Tata bathed Mama in the water." Ndadia throws a second stone. "Yet she grows weaker."

"Do you believe in it, Mom?" Gordie asks when his parents talk of *ndoki* in the village. His mother flushes and her forehead forms a horseshoe. "Of course not, Gordon. It's hocus pocus." Then she adds, "Just stay away."

At the close of this morning's final hymn, Gordie slipped out the church door past his mother's whisper, "Chicken and yams!" Eating wasn't on his mind. Anyway he prefers Mama's *fufu* and *mbika* to his own mother's criticism of the Sunday service. Gordie left his mother standing on the church step looking windblown and scornful, one large hand against her stomach. Her mighty pregnancy empowers her: his father brings her food and pillows. Gordie brings her drinks. Ndadia's been after Gordie's mother never to look at the village cripple who shuffles along on his backside, flip-flops on his hands. He crouches Sundays by Gordie's mother's pew, waits for *makuta* coins to fall.

Knows she will show compassion in public. It's a different story when schoolgirls stop by the house for a drink of fridge-cold water. His mother fixes them an icy stare and answers nothing, so that finally they back away, giggling and angry.

"If you look, the *nkita* will cause bad mischief to your baby, madame," Ndadia says. Ndadia says the cripple is a sorcerer paying for the crimes he performed through bad ancestors, those unwise while on earth. Gordie's mom smiles with her mouth but not her eyes and tells Ndadia the hour is late and he should run home for supper. Early in the pregnancy Mama sent Gordie's mother a thick-roped bracelet to wear, to make sure the baby comes out normal. Ndadia carried it the four kilometres dangling respectfully from his fingers, but Gordie's mother laid her large hand over the bracelet and said, "Ndadia. Return it."

Tata steps from the hut, squinting in sunshine, carrying a pail and basin. Maybe this afternoon Gordie and Ndadia will snap fish. Gordie's brought a joint along, hidden in his shorts.

Sleepy Sunday afternoons Ndadia and Gordie, Mama, Tata, and Ndadia's seven brothers laze beneath *lifaka* trees and drink *malafu*. Before Gordie goes home, Mama gives him a long-stemmed root to chew, to take the smell of palm wine away.

"*Masa*," Tata calls in the direction of Ndadia's brothers, who are passing a calabash of wine, and the monkey shrieks, swings from the tree, and hightails for the hole beneath the shed.

Tata returns, sets an empty Coke bottle and a large calabash on the hard courtyard dirt beside the pail and basin. Ndadia's oldest brother grunts and calls to the next oldest, "Fetch the water." That brother shifts in the heat, takes a gulp of *malafu* and calls, "Ndadia." And Ndadia drops his stone, and he and Gordie head for the containers. When his sister grows, Ndadia will order her, but for now her arms are too small to lift a full pail of water to her head.

Gordie places the pail within the basin and loads them on his head. Ndadia balances the Coke bottle in the wide neck of the calabash and does the same, then grabs two palm branches tied with nylon string from inside the hut. Gordie has two number sixteen fishhooks in a small pouch in his pocket. They set out down the red dust path toward the river.

"But it *is* Simbi!" Ndadia says the minute they start out, his legs dusted grey in churning heat. Eyes sorrowful. "Simbi." The sun so hot it hurts. "Simbi's jealous she does not have a fine husband like Tata. The ancestors told Tata last night in a dream." Sweat shines Ndadia's nose. Simbi. Mama's sister. The one unmarried woman in Lusekele. Mama's sister who lived a year in Canada where she studied at a nurse's college. Since she's returned to work at Vanga hospital, the villagers say a spirit possesses her. They know this because she cannot catch a husband. Gordie's mom says Simbi's too smart to fall for an uneducated village man, but the women only laugh.

The boys reach the river's edge and collapse in grass and dirt under the trees' dense shadow. When Gordie was kicked out of TASOK International School in Kinshasa last year for smoking dope, they sent him up-country to Milundu. That principal knew punishment. Three weeks of his parents' silent grim reproach. You'd think he'd had Slims Disease. But Ndadia. He was there to meet the Cessna when Gordie landed. Ndadia took him snap fishing at the river every afternoon, Ndadia held his head when Gordie cried. When your heart is aching turn to Jesus, Gordie's mother tells the village women. Gordie has no need for Jesus. He has Ndadia.

Somewhere, behind them, a parrot screeches. Gordie passed grade nine at TASOK International School, although he didn't make the honour roll, disgusting his parents once again. Ndadia dreams of going to the international school with Gordie, staying in the Baptist hostel, but his parents have no money, so in six weeks Gordie will leave Ndadia behind again and head for Kinshasa. Ndadia walks daily to Milundu school, four kilometres each way. At Milundu the teachers show up when they want to. Ndadia wrote exams last week. Zaire is out of paper, so the students copied questions off the shiny blackboards. Gordie asked his mother if he couldn't give Ndadia's class some of the paper stacked in his father's office.

His mother said, "Gordie, that wouldn't solve Zaire's problems!"

It would solve Ndadia's problem. Zaire needs Jesus, Gordie's mother says. Our Saviour can solve every problem.

The sun hangs low in the sky when Gordie and Ndadia fill the pail and basin with murky river water, and head through the sand for Ndadia's hut. The girl in the river mud last week whispered to Gordie, "I shall visit your home," and disappeared into the forest, trailing her mud-splashed clothes. The first time Gordie had a girl was last year after they expelled him. That girl also came to his house after, a Sunday evening, while his parents were in Vanga at the whites' church service. She didn't come back for sex. This one won't either. She came with a basket on her arm and searched his mother's cupboards, dropping into her basket canned beans, canned tuna, a half dozen muffins, a loaf of bread, a pineapple sitting on the cupboard. His mom and dad returned early and Gordie shoved the girl out the back door off his bedroom, sent her tripping in darkness over the hot water bucket, bumping the ash-filled burning-barrel. He listened for a week to his mom's astonished exclamations about his eating habits.

They walk slowly now, Gordie and Ndadia, through the oiled heat, pail and basin on their heads, sharing the marijuana. Then Ndadia says, "Boma."

It's a game he started years ago. Ndadia's travelled no farther than Vanga, but he knows geography.

"Boma."

"Ships and yellow hills," says Gordie.

"Moanda."

"Mist."

"Kimpese."

"Red African tulip trees."

"Canada." The boys look at one another. It's been five years for Gordie. Who could imagine.

"Mawa penja," Ndadia says, his voice stresses air, "what I long for more than life is Mama's health and a small notebook."

◼◤◥◆◤◥◼

Matondo Sunday today. Thanksgiving Sunday. Zaire's yearly sacrifice to God. An upsetting day, what with the women going wild. Vera enters the church on her husband's arm, followed by Gordie. She sets her heavy body on the backless bench. Three months to go. Some of those shameless girls turn, stare at her belly. Then the first hymn begins.

>*Diansambu diadi ekangu*
>*Mu zola tukangaziananga*

Eight verses if there's one. On the second verse Pastor Pambi raises his arms and already here come the mamas dancing their garden produce, their animal offerings, down the aisle. Vera's discussed this behaviour at women's prayer group. They don't need to be so suggestive with their bodies; they choose to be. Stan winces in disgust but Gordie's lapping it all in. The newly arrived missionary's wife says accept it, it's cultural. But then what can one expect, she's Lutheran. They don't even baptize properly. Of course it's cultural. It's cultural and wrong. The women giggling, now laughing outright, sure their sacrifice will outdo the men's. There goes Mama Lutantu, breasts bouncing in time to her oranges and grapefruit. Look at their swaying hips, clapping at the front while the men dance. Vera would like someone to tell her what this has to do with praising God.

Turning church into a circus. The baby hangs like a stone-filled apron in her lap. Cackling ducks, chickens, the village rooster, legs pinned together, quivering rabbits, a quilt of eggs, peanuts, beans, papaya, blanket the church platform. The front row worshipers clap at the goats breakfasting on the offering. What's the commotion? The village rooster. He's kicked himself free of the string that bound his legs, he's sailing through the window, and Pastor Pambi, hands undulating air, cries, "Praise for your resurrection, Lord."

It's so unworshipful.

Six women arrive today for Vera's cooking class. Only Mama Kiamfu is absent — at the Vanga mission hospital having her seventh baby. And she barely twenty-eight years old. Her two youngest have straight red hair, a sure sign of malnutrition. So how will she feed more? And of course Mama Kunda, at death's door with Slims Disease. Vera's heels hurt. Today they're cooking with bananas. Using the oven in the back yard, for really what's the point of teaching these women to use a stove they'll never own? They come, polite and head-dipping, but Vera can see contempt behind their eyes. The new missionary's wife told Vera she overheard the women saying, "The whites have so few babies because white babies come by luck. Each time they must figure out anew how it's done. Monsieur and Madame Hutchison took fifteen years to remember." And the young wife laughed. Gordie says nothing about the baby.

"Could we come to attention please. Today I'll demonstrate banana bread and banana cake. Bananas are a good source of potassium. We'll use palm oil instead of margarine. . . ." Already they're bored and shuffling, looking round Vera's kitchen, at her tins of relief food — MCC beef, at her chunk of South African cheese, her dirndl skirt laid on the ironing board. Their eyes miss nothing.

Vera sets out the measuring cups, the bowls. The women touch the glassware and chatter in Kituba, on purpose so she cannot understand. Vera divides the group in two. In the middle of her final instructions, just as she's handing out the powdered milk, there's a *"Ko-ko"* at her door. Two boys from the elementary school to get their drooping basketball pumped up. As if she has nothing else to do. When Vera returns, the women have mixed all the ingredients and she can tell by looking that they haven't measured.

"How much flour did you put in?"

They nod. "Eeeh."

"But did you measure carefully?"

"Eeeeeh."

"This will not work," Vera says, "because you were too careless with the measurements. Look at the recipe — see here — *two* cups?"

The women watch Vera. She gives up, waves them outdoors to carry their two pans of slopping batter to the old cook stove under the palm tree. Mama Lutantu lights a fire beneath it. They stay out in the back yard gabbing while Vera in her silent living room puts her aching feet up on the plastic ottoman and folds her hands over her stomach. The baby's still. They want her to offer them ice-cold water from her refrigerator, but if she does, she'll have ten more in cooking class tomorrow.

The back door opens. Vera watches the backs of Gordie's long stick legs beneath his cut-off shorts. His bare feet slip through the living room into Stan's office. A rustling. He sticks his head out, raises a notebook and his whispered voice holds a question. "Mom?"

Vera opens her eyes.

"I suppose that's for Ndadia," she says. "Firstly, Gordon, those notebooks are for Dad's workers to purchase. Secondly, we need to teach these people to work for what they get. You can't just give your things away." She closes her eyes against his blue ones.

Forty minutes in hot bleak sunlight and the women carry two overdone soggy-in-the-centre breads into the house. While Vera slices what should have been banana bread into neat squares, Mama Lutantu takes the knife, chops a rectangular section from the other's centre and offers it to Mama Luwenge, who cuts a hunky parallelogram for Mama Tumbu.

Vera closes with prayer.

Stan and Vera's Land Rover jolts down the rutted hill, over the creaking wooden bridge, through the thick sand up to Vanga village.

"Prepare ye, Prepare ye, Prepare ye the way of the Lord," Stan sings. "And the Saviour bears me gently, O'er the places once so rough." The baby rebels. The Land Rover stops dead at the clinic and by the time Vera has hoisted herself out, she can only see Stan's feet sticking out from under the vehicle.

"I'll need to check with Dudley if my supplies are in," Stan's voice says beneath the jeep. "I'll be back around three." Vera heaves herself, sweating, into the green-walled clinic and sits near the door. Simbi, dressed in her green nurse's uniform, is helping an old man hobble across the waiting room floor on a gangrenous foot. Vera's heel throbs. The other nurses, all men, circle wide around them.

"Madame Hutchison," Simbi says. A moment later, under thirty pairs of eyes, she shows Vera into Dr. Schappert's office.

"They stare at me because I have this baby, and at you, Simbi, because you don't," Vera says. Simbi's hair is combed into seven braided coils around her head. It's hard for Vera to believe, looking at Simbi, that she lived in America. Stan and Vera's Evangelical Renewal Baptist mission placed Simbi in a nursing college in Alberta. This ties them, somehow. Simbi must be back over a year.

"Monsieur Hutchison and I will shortly be commencing a preaching series called Oh the Peace the Saviour Gives that we'll take around to neighbouring villages. Perhaps you'll want to help." They could use Gordie's help as well, but Gordie is more interested in living like a native than being a personal witness. Simbi, her back to Vera, washes her hands at the sink and doesn't answer.

Vera sighs and says, "How's Mama Kunda?"

Simbi looks startled.

"She's very ill, madame." She bends low, examining the callouses on Vera's heels. "Simbi, my husband and I have heard ridiculous rumours." Simbi's cool fingers press into Vera's pulse. Her lips move. Counting.

"Gordie brings home a lot of silliness about the cause of Mama Kunda's illness." Vera stares at Simbi who has lifted Vera's dress and is kneading the skin of her vast stomach.

"When have you last felt movement from this baby?" Simbi asks.

"Oh heavens, not five minutes ago," Vera says. "In America no one dies of a curse. They have a name for Mama Kunda's illness in America. What's it called?"

"Slims Disease," says Simbi, looking in Vera's ears.

"Well, yes," Vera shifts on the table. "That's the African's name for it. I guess you couldn't learn everything during the fortunate time you spent in Alberta. Anyway, it's deadly, the disease. How old is Mama Kunda?"

"Forty-two."

"That's my age." Vera says. "It's not that I have anything against Mama Kunda." Simbi's long fingers begin to probe Vera's privates. "It's just what will our workers think with Gordie running off there every day, up to goodness knows what?"

"Slide down," Simbi says. She probes some more.

"That we favour Tata Kunda's family. That's what. Now you're a smart woman, Simbi." Vera pulls down her dress, her body humming pleasantly from all that touching. "Some day you'll find a lovely educated man who appreciates your smarts...."

"Why did you wait so many years to have this baby?"

How dare the woman meddle in her business. Simbi has come around the table and is looking at her. Vera speaks severely out the window where a July wind shakes leaves on the orange tree.

"Well, we chose to have one child, but the way things have turned out — God, seeing us as His worthy vessels, has now entrusted to us another."

Simbi smiles. She turns to the sink to scrub her hands. Vera stops thinking of Simbi at all. She closes her eyes, lies still and irritated, trying to bring back the humming. Why didn't Gordie just take the notebook if it's so important? He steals food for himself right from my kitchen, she thinks, but won't steal a notebook for a friend.

"Gordie always twists situations to look like our responsibility," Vera says to Simbi, but Simbi is gone.

Gordie and Ndadia reach Lusekele clearing in Zaire's quick-gathering dusk. The monkey streaks towards them over the hard-packed compound dirt, leaps into Ndadia's arms, clawing his shirt. Tata Kunda and Ndadia's brothers speed behind him.

"Grab him now. Hang on to Kiki," they call. Gordie and Ndadia lunge, bump heads as the monkey skids between Ndadia's legs. Gordie catches Kiki by a paw and the monkey squeals and hoots and scratches.

"What's happening?" Gordie asks. A brother brushes a skinned knee and says, "The monkey's stealing chicken eggs." Broken shells scatter the courtyard dirt. Tata has disappeared inside the makeshift shed. He steps out with his machete, and heads for the chopping block. Kiki screeches and tries to twist from Gordie's arms.

"Gordie. Come." Tata calls, and Gordie carries the scratching animal to the chopping block. Tata spreads Kiki's fingers against the block, lays Gordie's hand over the monkey's wrist, raises the machete. And as the small hand strains, curls against his, Gordie sees one finger is already cut off at the knuckle, the wound days old, scarred and infected.

⬙⬙⬙

In darkness, Tata draws a cross in the compound dirt, stirs in the cemetery mud he's fetched, mixed with palm wine, and pours it all into this indent. Scooping up the mud, he disappears into the hut to rub Mama's body. The monkey has not come out in hours from the hole beneath the shed. A thin dog appears and wails, eerie and shrill. Mama sleeps. Odours arise: the smell of unwashed body, death, herbs, and *saka-saka*.

"Ndadia, she will get better," Gordie says to his friend. The small sister watches from her grass mattress on the courtyard dirt. Ndadia's black face stretches suddenly, contorts over white teeth. And Gordie leaves him.

⬙⬙⬙

On Milundu compound, Vera, awake with discomfort from the lump of baby and the memory of Simbi's touch, reviews in her mind the song she and Stan will sing at their first outdoor Oh The Peace the Saviour Gives rally.

> "Only a little while, Of walking with weary feet,
> Patiently over the thorny way, That leads to the
> golden street."

Somewhere a cock crows.

KILLING TIME

Just this moment, on a warm Saskatchewan petunia-scented evening in May, a man dies. He is fifty-three years old. He has a son. The son is grief-stricken. He does not want this moment. His father's death confirms that time is in motion, he too will die. In the moments before his death, the father asks his son to open the night table drawer. From the drawer, the son extracts his father's watch. The watch has a large face, clear black numbers. It is a faithful watch, his father says, with this watch one knows exact time. The father dies. Saturday evening. Six-thirteen. The Saskatchewan son encloses the watch between his palms, and grieves.

Across the world, in the distant Zairian village of Kimpese, a boy hears the church bell toll. In Zaire, it is already Sunday morning. This boy smells drying manioc, colocassia and lemons. He hears a cock crow. The cry tells him it is time to rise for morning prayers. The boy pulls on his pants and goes to church.

In the next six years the son will put measured time between himself and his father's death. Between himself and Saskatchewan. During this time, he will go away to university, marry, travel to Africa, taking with him his father's watch. The

Kimpese boy will mail a letter to a departed missionary asking for school fees. He will build a fence for a *mundele*. He will herd cattle for an uncle.

In that hot distant land, the son's hand strays often to his father's watch face. The watch ticks on. He carries it with him everywhere. A walk among the baobabs. A quick shunt in the river. Hot wind bike rides. Muggy mornings in a stifling class-room. The son snatches glances, intimate readings of time's pas-sage. Sometimes he takes the band of his father's wristwatch in a finger, draws the crystal away from his skin. An unconscious brushing. He cannot pass a single day without its blessing. Even in the blackness of a Zairian night, his watch lying face up on the night table, time clings to him. Salty. Sweating. He lives his life divided. Half of him rushes to classes, marks students' papers, swims in CINAT pool, brushes his wife's hair. The other half watches himself, passing through time, his father's son. On his arm he wears his history and his future.

The Kimpese boy catches images of another world within his village. A transistor radio. A coiled necklace on a pale neck. Eggs delivered by the dozen. A silver comb and brush set. A motorcycle. A foreign language. Paper. Stacks of paper. A glass cup.

The son tells his physics students: Time marks the relation-ship between events in the real world. Time is constructed of isolated moments. Time exists when named. His students bow their heads and copy.

In the fury of a February rainstorm, a young man tears apart a door, timing the wrenching of boards against long thunder cracks. When the heavens explode with light, the thief slides his body against the bougainvillea bush and counts to four. It is an early Sunday morning. In a few hours, the thief will pull on dry clothes, and enter the brick steepled Kimpsese church as he has done since childhood. He twists his body through the crawl space, stands silent till the objects in the strange room take form.

His bare feet brush the *mundeles'* cement floor. He does not hurry. No one has taught him that time is of the essence.

Lightening claws the sky. The undersides of the thief's feet catch the light, frozen, frozen, frozen in time, the thief steals through the *mundeles'* silent bedroom, squats in darkness, admires the watch with a careless lack of fear while the *mundeles'* breaths somersault into the air. The thief slips the watch into his trouser folds. Draws in the sleeping man's breaths. Disappears.

To the east, in the low branches of a *lifaki* tree, the village rooster, drenched, exhausted by his dreams, cocks his head, shakes out his feathers, stretches proudly, gathers himself to crow.

For the moment, time, in motion, flutters on.

THE THIEF

The day before the thief broke in, Paul stood in the doorway of his physics classroom, waiting for Kisungu, still copying her homework off the blackboard. In the sky the sun was a dim circle behind a thin layer of cloud. Kisungu wore her blue skirt and a white slip top which she believed was a blouse. Paul contemplated pointing out the inappropriateness of a slip top as an outer garment. Then he briefly considered offering Kisungu physics help at his house after siesta, but Kisungu might steal his pens. So he stood silent, waiting to walk across the grass-clumped soccer field, step into the dimness of their tin-roofed house at the compound's edge and change into shorts. Rita would be working on lessons at her desk before their iron-barred den windows, Emmanuel padding silently about the kitchen, baking peanuts and grinding them into peanut butter. By noon, the crisp smell of peanut butter cookies would skim Paul's nostrils and for a brief moment, he'd imagine himself right out of this dusty village. The rancid manioc smell, the sweating bodies, the tear-jerking sharpness of *pili-pili,* he'd order into a drawer in his mind, and push it shut.

Kisungu sat with one foot flung carelessly into the aisle, like she was trying to air out, while Paul sweated politely in his white cotton pants and khaki shirt. Paul found it hard to believe this was the middle of February. He imagined the banana trees laced with fresh white snow, the high green grasses crushed flat by ice. Already the clouds were beginning to thicken. The only change this country offered — rain or no rain. Green-green or brown-green. Time moved, but not ahead. Sometimes Paul panicked, believed they would never escape Zaire, that two years would pass in Canada, but their moment here would last forever.

Kisungu gathered her books together, made an "Eiiiiiiiii," and said, "C'est trop, Monsieur." Kisungu wasn't smart, but she no longer brushed her body against Paul's when she skipped off the step and headed for the girls' dorm. Some things she'd learned. The white man lives by order. Paul watched her go, her yellow thongs, flip-flops, as they called them, an extension of her walk.

Paul walked the straight, flat length of soccer field into the grove of trees where some of the boys had dragged school desks and were studying in the shade. Biyini was there, small against the giant ironwoods. He propped his bare foot against a tree, toes spread wide like tree toads hanging on a wall. Paul glanced at Biyini's distended cheek, its flaring cut. The spirit of Mavambu's ancestors beat him, Biyini said, for not paying back the ten zaires he owed. When Paul asked what he meant by that, Biyini doggedly repeated. Mavambu had beat him up in spirit. His ancestors did the job. Six roommates bore a solemn witness. They'd watched him try to dodge the invisible blows. *Ndoki,* monsieur, they told Paul, eyes shielding fright. Witchcraft. Paul felt another headache coming on.

Paul stepped into the warm darkness of the cement kitchen, poured himself a glass of lime juice, and walked straight through to the den. Rita was wearing a blue-checked sundress. Her small body glistened like oil beneath it. At intervals she rubbed her

THE COCK'S EGG

bare feet across the cement floor to cool them. Paul liked how
Rita looked, so organized among her books, her face posed in
concentration. He knew Zairian men found Rita scrawny, unat-
tractive. They liked beefy women. This knowledge put Paul at
ease. He didn't like the worry of having to fight for Rita's honour. If it hadn't been so beastly hot, Paul might have suggested
an afternoon in bed. But then what would they do at eight that
night? Sitting too close to the Aladdin lamp made the heat
unbearable. Not sitting close enough made reading the Reader's
Digest Condensed books they'd found stacked in the pantry an
impossibility. To make things worse, a varied collection of bugs
and moths and unknown swooping insects, frantic for the light,
threw themselves against the lamp, singed their wings to stink-
ing stumps, and fell gyrating on the open page. This happened
every evening until Paul and Rita gave up, shooed the cockroaches out of the bathroom, washed up in the granite basin,
checked the bedroom walls for termite tunnels, and crawled
into bed.

"I can't believe it!" Rita said, chewing designs into her pen.
"Musungu and Lungiambudila cheated again!" Cheating gained
definition with Paul and Rita's arrival in this village seven
months ago. Before, a gift of money or a Western shirt from the
boys, sex from the girls, turned the teachers' heads the other
way. With fifty students to a classroom, three students to a desk,
one would have thought a war on cheating futile. But Paul and
Rita were winning. Students like Kisungu tried their tactics on
Paul only once, then learned to sit curled over test papers, dusty
feet stuck out into the aisles. True, some students became inven-
tive. Rita found entire English conversations in shorthand
scratches on brown palms. Paul discovered a boy crouched in his
desk, reading physics equations off the inside of his thong.

"I just can't believe it!" Rita said. There were a lot of things
Paul just couldn't believe. The school year starting shakily
almost five weeks late, the discipline director's cruel punish-

ments, the village women's carolling giggles whenever they looked at Rita.

The afternoon before the thief broke in, a thunderstorm brewed. Clouds rolled in at alarming speed, packaging in grey the wide blue space, while the air turned yellow, ethereal; stilled. A swishing started in the palm trees, louder, louder, until their branches bent low and swept paths in the red dirt with their fronds. Thunder boomed in long staccato cracks. The sky began to rush in on them, cold. Mangos bounced to the ground and lightning split the grey. Students ran for cover while Paul and Rita stood outside and watched.

"Allez vous cacher, monsieur!" Hide yourself! The sky is falling! They flew like chickens, frantic to find cover. It's the ancestors of an enemy, reaching out to kill you! they told Paul when he discussed the concept of lightning in class. Huge slow drops splattered the dirt. An ancestor spitting his contempt, Paul thought. An explosion of thunder and the compound became an instant blur, like unfocussed binoculars. Rain coursed from the sky, battered blossoms off flame trees, dug trenches in the path beside their door. Guinea fowl flapped miserably under its lancing punishment while orange and brown lizards skittered beneath the house. Paul saw himself whipped in the wind, on the cover of *National Geographic*. He could have wrung his clothes out like a sponge.

Rain gushed through their open windows, the cement floors snaked rivulets. Paul and Rita laughed and slid like lizards on waxed linoleum as they shut the banging windows and lit the coal oil lamp. Paul felt himself fill with an unnerving happiness, the throbbing of the night a physical sensation that entered his pores. They left their bedroom curtains open and the air rose steamy out their window, like translucent fog, enveloped the smell of peanut butter cookies and Rita's sweat. Paul could still taste the tartness of the pineapple slices that cut Rita's lips at supper. He touched her and she shivered, uncovered in the heat, but let him stroke the tension from her back and thighs until she too rose to the tempo of the storm. When at last they fell asleep, their sheets felt sodden in the dark air, and the rain was hollow-sounding, like the striking of gourd drums.

The next morning under grey sky full of rain, they found their slatted door all ripped apart. Pried-off wood slats strewed their cement floor; an iron bar lay on the porch.

"How could this have happened while we slept!" Paul said and fought the spot of fear that welled inside his stomach. He walked from room to room, incredulous. Rita's bicycle gone, Paul's black umbrella, bought in Belgium, their Nikon zoom lens camera, the short wave radio, their dirty clothes left in the hamper in the hall, Rita's cloth shoulder sack, and Paul's Seiko watch.

The thief had left the desk drawers partly open in the den. They looked a mess. Paul straightened each and shut them carefully.

"He took my best dress!" Rita said.

"Those bloody sons of bitches!" Paul said. "I guess we call the préfet. Maybe you should go," Paul said to Rita. "You can't stay here alone."

"The thief's long gone," Rita said. "I'm not afraid to stay."

Ankle deep in mud, Paul slogged his way to Citoyen Kinkela's house. His flip-flops splashed mud to his thighs. The farther he left his house behind, the more anger replaced fear. The citoyen was most apologetic, most alarmed.

"If this thief is not found, if our things are not returned," Paul said, "we will be looking for a different placement!" The préfet nodded, careful and polite. A gendarme was summoned, a short squat man who arrived two hours late, sweating in his army uniform. He and Citoyen Kinkela dashed about the house, examined the non-existent items, made disappointed "ahhhhh" sounds at each site. Paul knew the power in his threat. A white man gave the school credibility. A government school would go to almost any lengths to keep *mundeles.* The préfet spoke to the gendarme in Kikongo, had Paul list again their missing items while the gendarme jotted nervously on his small notepad.

Rumours abounded on the compound. The thief was a local gendarme's brother. In a neighbouring village, a white missionary's house was broken into. Her sentinel was killed. She, hacked up by machetes. A gang of thieves was hiding up the Bangu. Kisungu's mother's uncle had spied them by the falls. The thief had used a magic potion (in spray form) to drug the white man and his wife into deep sleep. The thief was student Diawambanzila's ancestor, reaping revenge on Paul for calling his great-great grandson fainéant.

Paul refused to go to class, stayed home all day to guard his ripped-up door. Demanded men come from the local carpenter shop to fix it.

"Certainement!" the préfet said. "Tout de suite!"

Two men arrived within the hour.

"J'ai soif!" the young one said abruptly before he'd worked ten minutes.

"I'll get you a drink of water," Paul said.

"Non," the man said, "Je veux du Coca!" Coke! Paul and Rita hadn't tasted Coke since their holiday to the capital at Christmas.

"I don't believe it!" Rita said. She handed him a glass of water, pushed it at him, defying him not to drink. He drank and worked in sullen silence.

"Nous partons maintenant," the quiet one said hours later. Paul inspected their work.

"But this is worse now than before you came!" he said. They had unscrewed the padlock to get the new door on. They failed to leave a space to put a door knob. Although they'd gone to great lengths to measure the door frame, over half an hour by Rita's watch, the door was one inch too short and several centimetres too wide and if not held in place, swung loose on its hinges. Paul felt his blood race round his heart and shoot to all nerve endings.

"Now we have no protection at all! You've even taken off the padlock!" Snorting in disgust, he slammed out to find the préfet who spoke quickly in Kikongo. The sullen one answered just as rapidly. Paul got the impression he was swearing. The quiet one stood and looked at Paul, his face expressionless, until Paul felt uneasy, like the man was seeing something in him.

The men worked on past darkness. Paul lit the lamp and moved it near the door, but neither man acknowledged it. When they left, Paul worked until ten o'clock, installing a second padlock that he found in the pantry, crusted with cockroach eggs. Before he went to bed, he piled six empty cans in a pyramid on the kitchen stool, made a loop around the pile with a piece of string, and tied it to the new doorknob.

"We won't be caught sleeping if the thief comes back!" Paul said.

◥◣◢◤◥◣◢◤

The morning after the thief broke in was market day in the village centre. Paul watched colleagues and students with a detective's air. If they smiled and said, "Bonjour, monsieur," he read it as a subtle smirk and answered curtly. He looked at the clothes of those who passed by on the path leading down the hill. And all the while, he arranged scenarios behind his eyes: Emmanuel tiptoeing stealthily across familiar floors, butcher knife in hand. Kisungu and her girlfriends darting out the slatted door, popping up his black umbrella, trailing Rita's underthings.

When they arrived at market, a wide cluster of gloomy stalls that smelled like *fufu* and decaying meat, they wandered in and out, mud clinging to their sandals until their feet became almost too heavy to lift. Rita picked her way between the stalls, she knew what she was looking for, and tucked palm oil soap and some *biteke-teke* under her arm. Paul scanned the market place. That's how he saw the bicycle, glinting in the sunlight. It looked like Rita's — new, a little tool pouch on the back — but painted black, where Rita's bike was green. Paul kept the man in sight, paced him along the rows of overripe tomatoes, *mbika* wrapped in manioc leaves, the yellow gourds cut into bowls. A group of goats and children gathered around Paul. The boys wore dirty shirts that flapped too large. One child was busy hiking up torn shorts.

"Mundele, donne moi l'argent!" the children shouted in hoarse, gleeful calls, moving dance-like between Paul and the bike, which now lay in the mud while the man tried on a bright red toque at a market stall. When the man picked up the bike and looped his leg over, Paul made a rush to read the identification. A frightened goat bayed loudly, scattering the children. The women at the stalls laughed and screamed words, their voices sharp bursts. Their gangly shoulders shoved and jerked in imitation. The people buying gathered round and laughed and imitated too. Paul, face blazing, watched the man ride by, grin and call out, *"Songonene, mundele!"* The wheels, Paul saw, were the thin kind, the toolcase hard black plastic.

"Did you see?" he said to Rita. "Didn't he grin in clear unease? Wasn't he the first to look away? You can bet that he knows something." They left the shrill women in the market stalls, and slipping in their sandals, flinging mud, made toward the hill that wound up to the compound. The children ran behind them shouting, *"Mundele,* donne-moi l'argent!"

They ate a lunch of squashed tomatoes and canned tuna ordered from South Africa. The kitchen collected heat in the airless room.

"I hate this place," Rita said. Paul sank his teeth into a tuna sandwich with suppressed rage.

"They're probably dividing up our things right now at the

gendarmerie!" he said. He was reaching for the margarine when they heard the frenzied clash of voices in the yard. Paul scraped his chair back on the cement floor, making Rita jump. Out the living room window, he saw a beat-up yellow jalopy. Every person in the village, adult and child, was crowding into their yard. They had a festive air, the suppressed excitement of children at the zoo. As Paul watched, a gendarme, his movements quick, excited, climbed out from behind the wheel, and opened up the trunk. He dragged a man out, arms tied behind his back, a thick brown rope around his neck. The crowd pressed up against each other, made noises in their throats as the gendarme led the roped man past Paul's window. Emmanuel, who joined Paul and Rita at the window, said, "Je crois c'est notre voleur," and brushed his hand in small, excited scratches at his face. Someone banged and shouted *"Ko-Ko"* at their door. Emmanuel's bare feet made soft slaps, and he opened the door wide, letting in a rush of wet smoke smell.

"Voilà, votre voleur!" the gendarme said. His face shattered in a circle of proud wrinkles. And Paul thought, what do I say, thank you very much? Invite them in?

The gendarme jerked the roped man forward. He tripped on the step and his fuzzy head bumped Rita on the thigh. Rita backed away, convulsed by shivers, and the crowd cried, "Eiiii, Eiiiii, Eiiii," and laughed. Kisungu, near the front, watched Paul, bold and parrot-like.

"Voilà, votre voleur," the gendarme said again and handed Paul the pistol, barrels first.

Paul's stomach clawed inside him, and he said, "Oh . . . no!" and scrunched his back against the wall as if he were the prisoner. The people shrieked with laughter. The thief's eyes flicked sideways at him, quick, like a viper's tongue, dull, almost uninterested, the eyelids puffy. The man's flesh was open where the cement step scraped him. It didn't bleed, but flecked red-grey.

The gendarme's fist caught the thief on the mouth and

knocked him to his knees. He struggled to his feet again, and stood, quivering, head turned away from Paul, skin already rising in a soft welt. The gendarme dropped his outstretched fist and made a little ticking in his teeth.

Paul saw Rita looking at the thief, his muscular legs, his sinewy, taut shoulders.

"Did you find our things?" she said.

"Qu'est-ce qu'il a pris?"

"Our bicycle. . . ."

The gendarme moved to face the thief, spoke quickly in Kikongo and cracked the man's breastbone, a sharp blow with the pistol stalk. The man drew up his shoulders and made a small sound, like the clearing of a throat. The crowd gave high wild-sounding yips. Kisungu and her friends began to dance. The thief's arms were tightly tied behind his back, Paul noticed suddenly, in Paul's CANADA T-shirt — tied at the elbows which fused his shoulders so he could not protect his body from the beating. His forehead, musty-smelling at this close range, was lined with beads of sweat. They were attractive beads that didn't run into the corners of his mouth and drop onto the ground as Paul's did. Instead they lined his forehead in straight rows, as if he had been primped to look hot for a movie.

"The camera. . . ." Rita said. This time the thief's face went tight with pain before the blow. Rita drew a breath and said, "I can't believe this," in an awful voice. "Our radio. . . ."

Paul stood beside his wife, imprisoned in the vision of the crowd, looking, he knew, white and senseless. He focussed on a tiny pinkish scar on the man's chest. It caught the sunlight. So did the wiry, tufted hairs that grew beside it.

"And then my shoulder sack. . . ." Rita said.

The thief's head jerked and Paul reached out his arms instinctively because he thought the man might fall. This made the students laugh again. The gendarme spoke in harsh Kikongo, put his hand on the thief's head and shoved him to his knees. The man was so close Paul could have reached out and touched his welted cheek. The thief answered, head bowed, voice guttural and low.

"Il dit il a ces choses," the gendarme said. "Qu'est-ce qui manque encore?" This time the gendarme looked at Paul.

Paul felt dizzy, surrounded by close-pressing human walls and a blue ceiling. The light cloud cover had separated into wisps, like tiny trails of cooking smoke. It made the sky look cheerful, decorated. Paul needed to run, but the world, tilting round him in sickening slow motion, willed him stationary. The gendarme watched Paul's face. Paul saw the people as a coloured blur viewed through a rainstorm. He smelled the acrid sweat of the kneeling man, and perhaps the sharp scent of *pili-pili*.

"Uh — my umbrella," he said, "and my watch that's all."

"Nous cherchons maintenant vos affaires," the gendarme said at last. "Peut-être vous pourriez me passer de l'argent pour le voyage à son village?"

"The préfet of the school," Paul said, "is responsible for any expenses."

Jerking on the rope, the gendarme led the prisoner away. The thief fell off the porch steps face down in the dirt, his shoulders wrenching. The gendarme kept walking, yanking on the rope. The thief scrambled on his knees and chest, twisted his body in the gravel and pulled himself along. The crowd began to howl and some of the grade twelve boys, Diawambanzila, Mavambu, Bayangelele, did taunting kicking dances in his path. When the thief tried to twist his body free, they kicked him in the ribs and stomach, striking hard dull blows with their bare feet.

Paul's mouth was so dry he could hardly swallow. The préfet threw quick, worried glances at him.

"Les *mundeles* n'aiment pas tout ça."

The gendarme shrugged, a contemptuous slight raising of the shoulders, but he waited while the thief swayed to his feet. When Paul caught a last glimpse, the gendarme was shoving the man back into the trunk, and then the lid slammed shut. The jalopy jerked away through muddy ruts, followed by a crowd that whooped and sang, banging a tinny drumbeat on the trunk. Kisungu's hands flashed brown-black to the rhythm.

The evening after the thief broke in, the men returned, this time in a truck. Rita's bicycle, scraped, a fender missing, was tied in the back. The thief sat beside it. His torso was set at an unnatural angle from his waist. His arms, still tied at the elbows, were puffy now, fluid collected under skin. He had begun to shake, a faint, but steady shimmer, like the fever that accompanies malaria. On his left side lay Paul's shortwave radio, without the cord, some clothes, and Rita's sack. Citoyen Kinkela rushed about the truck, unloading things. A village rooster, irritated, stalked, buck-buck-bugocking across the road. Paul felt a sudden need to communicate with the thief. He stared, but the thief sat, shoulders jolted back, eyes averted, as if Paul weren't worth his time.

"What will happen now?" Rita asked as the gendarme crawled in behind the wheel. He made a horizontal gesture near his throat and that little clicking sound.

"What do you mean?" Rita said.

"On va l'éliminer," the gendarme said.

"But surely that's not necessary!" Paul said.

"Oui," the gendarme said and drove away.

The day after the thief broke into Paul and Rita's house, Citoyen Kinkela came hurrying through the brief dusk that

THE COCK'S EGG

shifts over an African sky.

"Voici votre montre, monsieur," he said. "Le voleur a été baïonnetté sur le pont ce soir. Je regrette beaucoup de vous causer tel de dérangement. Tout va bien maintenant?" His face was a hopeful question mark.

The Seiko ticked its time into the gloom. Paul held it in his hands (it smelled of sweat and *pili-pili)* and watched the moist black curtain blotting out the shimmering leaves of the acacia tree.

"Surely they didn't kill him!" Rita said.

"They seem to think they had no choice," Paul said. "What a fucking stupid man to wear my shirt!"

The night air was so muggy Paul found it hard to breathe. He strapped his watch on angrily. It pinched his arm hairs. He took it off again, "I just can't stand this heat!" he said and headed for the kitchen where he leaned his back against the cupboard, drew in the scent of peanut butter cookies Emmanuel had baked, fresh that morning, and for one sparing moment imagined himself right out of Africa. When he opened his eyes, the outline of the forest out the kitchen window looked dark and endless, a solid wall.

COMPOS/URE

I'll cut last night's scene here in Kinshasa, where I cook dinner in your apartment on the guest house compound, avocados stuffed with tuna imported from South Africa, where-I'm wearing my peasant dress and sandals that wrap up my ankles, and my Ce Soir perfume and you don't show because, you say this morning, you bumped into friends from Mbandaka at the American Club and it got late, well, there are no telephones.

I'll cut the funny story you told, expecting me to laugh: while you partied with your friends at the Memling Bar (I waiting in your empty room), a guy tried to steal your money. You grabbed his hand, still attached to your back pocket, and the man holding your hand bellowed, Ce n'est pas moi!

I'll cut your joyous, carefree, Fuckez-vous! to the gangs of small boys who surround your Land Rover at N'jili airport.

I'm going to cut a lot of scenes to make this story. I won't be in my bedroom in Kimpese with the curtains drawn, my fingers trembling. Waiting for your letter, for your word. Afraid Zaire's white light will infiltrate that space behind my eyes. Explode my reason. Afraid of silence. Afraid of you.

Okay. Here goes.

You drive me to the baseball game, Mennonites versus Baptists, and buy us hot dogs from the vendeurs beside TASOK pool. I watch the rhythm of your long legs slide away from me, the way you jerk your head to throw hair from your eyes.

Waiting for your return, I climb the bleachers. (I wait for you a lot these two weeks in Kinshasa.) These grandstands have such gaps between the seating planks. A person could fall through. A rooster clucks below the bleachers, gorging himself on grubs. I scan the sky, that blue-white backdrop to the baseball players. Green grass. White white bases. A yellow bucket of baseballs. Brown wood bats. Crayon drawing of a perfect world here in Kinshasa. Friends say you've screwed expatriate women from Kijiji to Kataka-Kombe.

Flashback. Christmas holidays at Vista. I wander to the beach. The wind is cool. I take the hundred or so stairs that follow down a yellow cliff to the blue Atlantic, swish my feet through rippling waves, step around a mangrove thicket's shadow, see a woman kissing you.

Forget flashback. I'll stitch the ball game in last. Start at the beginning with your invitation to skip down from Kimpese for the holidays. Renew our "friendship." Stay at your apartment. Untouched dinner. No. This story will not write itself.

A woman at the ball game declares her presence. She has a mongoose. Attached to a long string. A miserable thing, it runs at you and nips your ankles. The woman, a teacher at the international school, yanks the string and calls, Go for it, Gooseberry! Give the scoundrel what he deserves. You laugh. She laughs. You wink. A woman in the bleachers eating mangoes confides that last week she saw your Land Rover parked outside the teacher's house till four in the morning.

Perhaps I'll focus on the weather. In this story the sun scorches, white. The humid air carries the delicate odour of the Congo, mixed with hot dogs and Zairian beer. Tired wives are cheering for their Baptist or their Mennonite. Yet, it's quieter here than in the cité where noise is music. Behind the cheers a steady hum vibrates — invisible insects, likely sand fleas. They prick skin prick skin prick skin, and a person doesn't notice. But suddenly, when it's too late, the body already damaged, the discomfort is too real to bear.

I'm wearing my bathing suit beneath my shorts and T-shirt. TASOK pool, which is behind the change rooms and cannot be seen from here, glistens blue.

We all come from somewhere else. You are American. I am Canadian — which pleases you. Although you'd like me better if I were Swiss. The back-catcher is a Swede. His wife is Belgian. It's May, a dry day for Kinshasa. You return with three hot dogs. You have forgotten I don't like ketchup. You spread your napkin, stretch your legs and, mouth full, ask if I watched baseball as a kid. I say, Canadians watch hockey.

You bite into the skin of your hot dog.

How about a backrub, you say.

Imagine. Christmas morning at Vista on the ocean. I walk until I can't see the guest houses any more and sit on a lone piece of driftwood that's dug itself into the sand. I watch the sideways sand crabs scuttling the shore. Just sit and taste hot sea breeze. You come walking down the beach, you haven't combed your hair. You nudge me over. After a bit you step behind me, begin to rub my shoulders. I steal into another form, become an army ant, imagine yellow pebbles, big as boulders, towering grasses, my body stroked by wind.

Needles of pain spike up my neck. I lay aside my food and rub your neck, dig into muscle, stretch fingers down your lean backbone.

I ask what plant is growing at the edge of the ball diamond. Spanish bayonet, you say.

Like us, it's been imported.

Just this moment, a Baptist hits a home run.

I look beyond the ball game to the thin dry season haze that holds Kinshasa.

I am writing my own failure.

SPANISH BAYONET. SPANISH DAGGER. *(Yucca aloifo-lia)*. Semi-desert plants of the lily family. Yuccas are cultivated for their striking flower clusters. The name comes from its sharp pointed leaves which are bayonet and dagger-tip: sharp and hard. Native uses for the plant: needle and thread combined.

The mongoose woman swings her ponytail back into the story, and even while I compose her out, she invites you to the pool. Only one character clings to this narrative, fragmented, vanishing. The game's in the fourth inning. Tied at two. You ease your shoulders back, say, Ah, there's the rub. This game is slow. A swim would be perfect now. You want another hot dog? You drop me two zaire.

The Linguala language has no future tense.

I can't transform this text.

My un-character ties her mongoose to the bleachers and you and she disappear into the change rooms. You've left behind your T-shirt. Despite the heat, I slip into its balled softness, store up your fragments.

In several minutes you and the mongoose woman will enter TASOK pool.

Which is very blue.

And cannot be seen from here.

The words I haven't written.

Prick skin. Prick skin. Prick skin.

I focus on the striking flower clusters of the Spanish dagger. Their sharp leaves point a bayonet right through my smile.

AN AUTHENTIC KENYAN HOLIDAY

- buy bra
- hand in list of students who passed and failed pour
  les délibérations
- bundle up old clothes et donné à Ndelo
- do a breast check
- ready titulaire folder for préfet
- give Mama leftovers en frigo

Velma came across this list of errands scrambling in her purse for gum, just as the huge breast of Mt. Kenya peeked through the clouds. Its glaciers shone blue and white light.

"Farmers grow coffee on the lower slopes. It's an extinct East African volcano with two peaks," Alicia said, her nose in her guidebook. That was Alicia. Reading off facts and missing the real thing. "The peak, Kibo, is the highest point on the African continent." The plane groaned and hovered.

"Everything's so blue up here," Velma said. Do Kenyans do maintenance on airplanes?

"The cheerful heart makes its own blue sky," Alicia warbled, smiling at the passengers. Velma gritted her teeth, dropped the crumpled list into the seat pocket in front of her, and chewed in time to the small explosions in her ears.

Velma had been travelling with Alicia for exactly one day. Eighteen to go. The idea for the trip started when Velma and Alicia both arrived in Kinshasa for Easter break. Alicia from Kijiji, Velma from Kimpese. A hot afternoon at the American Club, over hamburgers and frites. Velma could conjure up the day, the brilliant cheerless sunshine, the burnt nut smell. Alicia was wearing a V-necked blouse. Her body small and muscular, pointy breasts. Velma sat beside her, a large and sweaty bulk. Velma had just arrived that morning from Kimpese, still reliving a scene from her English classroom, not yet having shaken work from her shoulders. Her first day of Easter vacation. What colour is your shirt? she was asking in her head. And Mbongombashi answering, Mees, she green. When, out of nowhere, Doug Markum appeared. His hair had grown and was brushed back on both sides into a rooster tail.

"Going anywhere for summer vacation, Velma?" Doug said. Expats flowed around them. Everyone tanned and happy. When Doug slipped his long legs around the fancy patio chair, his knee brushed hers. Velma's mouth would have gone dry, but it was full of frites, and when she tried to indicate this, she felt a spray of mush escape between her teeth. Doug's blue eyes melted into her own and her voice came out too shrill, "Well, I'm thinking of Kenya." The possibilities! Doug Markum and Kenya. Mombasa and Doug. Doug and sugar beaches. That she was six years older than Doug wouldn't mean a thing.

"Kenya. Good idea," Alicia said. "Are you considering company?" She winked at Velma.

"Well," Velma murmured. Her cheeks burned. She couldn't look at Doug. His fingers slid by as he stole a frite.

"Consider me in," Alicia said.

"Great frites, Velma," Doug said, and she blushed again as if she'd created them herself.

"If it isn't Doug Markum," a woman cried and Doug unwound his legs and sailed off into the crowd. Velma breathed. In. Out.

"When should we leave?" Alicia asked.

"We just got here," Velma said.

"No silly, I mean for Kenya!" Alicia giggled.

Doug was nowhere in sight.

The plane lurched, heavy and ponderous in its descent, and the engines droned. Velma looked now at Alicia. Curly blonde hair. Pert breasts stabbing through her blouse. Velma hardly knew her. Alicia was looking down at Velma's shoes. Velma bought new shoes for this trip, multicoloured, teal and orange and pink. She'd thought they would match anything, but it turned out the opposite. She owned no orange clothes; the pink and teal so bright her sundresses looked drab.

"Interesting shoes, Velma," Alicia said. "You're not usually so colourful." Velma's new bra was white. Eye-punishing white. Her first new bra in a year, the other so soaked in sweat it smelled garlicky, even freshly washed and hanging to dry in sunshine. Alicia was younger than Velma by five years, but Velma had seen no way out of the travel arrangement, and the trip seemed preferable to a month at Baptist Bible Camp. The British Baptists at Kimpese usually manipulated Velma to work in their mosquito-infested high school Bible camp. One of their numerous self-inflicted punishments.

The runway raced to meet them and the plane thumped down.

THE COCK'S EGG

Velma and Alicia stepped over sunbaked dirt and through the post office door. The post office smelled of damp wood and dirty papers. Kenyan men formed a row behind them, clutching letters and small packages, or waiting empty-handed.

"Dancing is a favourite form of recreation in Kenya," Alicia read. She paused, looked up, as if she expected the row of Kenyan men to break into a line dance.

The two women stood behind a tall blond American. His hair waved slightly.

"Hi," Alicia said. She was in her olive dress with a wide skirt that swirled about her knees. The American nodded. He waited behind a short moist-faced Kenyan who held a twine-wrapped package. The Kenyan shoved his parcel across the counter.

"Kenya's coastal area is humid and tropical. Sandy beaches, lagoons, and patches of rain forest line the coast."

Velma's skirt stuck to her buttocks. Her thighs stuck to each other. She needed a shower. Velma wanted to be at the train station, ensuring two seats to Mombasa and the Indian Ocean. But Alicia had friends who sent her letters. Two hours into Kenya and she had to check for mail. Velma would shower tomorrow when they booked into the Sun and Sand Hotel. Alicia's choice, the Sun and Sand Hotel. The brochure said, a lovely ocean setting amidst coconut palms and white sand. An authentic Kenyan holiday. Book now. The Sun and Sand was farther up the coast.

"If this line moves," Alicia said, "we can catch the night train to Mombasa." Pamphlets sprawled from her fingers. Bamburi. White Sands. The touristy hotels Velma would have chosen. "In the morning we'll jump a *matatu*," she looked proudly at the Kenyan men around her, "and be at the Sun and Sand by noon."

Twenty hours, then Velma could shower. In the shower she would be alone. The rushing water would spray away her irritation, drown out Alicia's cheerful voice.

"Most Kenyan men wear a cotton shirt and shorts or trousers. The women wear cotton dresses or skirts and blouses."

"Any mail for Krieger?" The American swung his green canvas shoulder bag from his arm, undid the clasp, and laid it on the counter.

"Some rural Kenyans, especially nomads, wrap a piece of cloth round their bodies for clothing." Alicia winked at Velma. "What did I tell you. We're going to see the real thing."

"*Ngojeya*," the clerk said. "First things first." The American pushed his ID and three shillings across the counter. The clerk handed him a letter and the American dropped it in his sack.

"*Mwa ngine*," the clerk said.

"Leedahl," Alicia said, "L-e-e-d-a-h-l." The clerk reached into a stack of mail and handed Alicia six letters. Velma had none.

The moist-faced Kenyan, passing Velma, flicked out his arm, snatched the American's shoulder sack, and sped out the door. Alicia shrieked. Velma smelled burnt charcoal and sunlit leather.

Piled voices. Texture of language. *Wewe!* What the hell! *Msima mishe huyo mtu!* Sons of bitches! *Una sanya nini!* Feet scuffling in the doorway. *Ta-adhari!*

The American's heels hit dirt outside the doorway. People spilled behind him, fanned out.

Velma pushed through the bodies, stuck her head into the street. The air burned hazy with roasting charcoal. Two figures sprinted in the distance. Kenyans pursued the American who pursued the thief. The thief glanced back, exerted a surprised burst of speed, flung the knapsack to the ground. The American bypassed it, sped on.

"Let's help!" Alicia cried. Velma jogged behind her, skirt clinging to her hips. Alicia reached the knapsack, dropped to her knees and gathered the spilled contents: two smushed papaya, a Swiss Army knife, a pair of khaki shorts, a letter.

Velma drew up behind her, breathing hard.

The American rounded the corner from an alley, dragging the Kenyan, bleeding from the mouth.

"I am sorry at my utmost," the man said in careful English. His frightened smile panned the crowd.

Alicia smiled back. "He's wearing cotton," she whispered to Velma.

"Too sorry. Please. I beg you. Do not call police." The thief did an odd pathetic quick bend of the knees, a curtsy. A tooth hung against his lip.

The American gave Alicia a curt nod when she handed him his knapsack ripe with smushed papaya. He took it with his free hand, the other looped around the small man's neck.

"You all right?" Alicia asked the thief who looked up at his captor, as if seeking the answer.

"I have children," he said to Alicia.

"Anything we can do?" Alicia asked.

"Where is the police station?" the American said. Alicia riffled through her pamphlets. The thief hawked, choking on his sobs.

A long distance away, Velma could see the bored post office clerk, his room now deserted, crouched in the doorway, gnawing on a twig.

◢◣◥◤◢◣

At eight o'clock, Velma and Alicia boarded the night train to Mombasa. Although they'd paid second class, Alicia found an unclaimed apartment, with two long wooden seats that sprang into beds, and a small corner sink. Velma set her reused bottle of warm orange soda on the floor, stowed her luggage above her head, and settled against the window with her drink. On the grass beside the train, a monkey ran at playing children. A black man, his white wife and three beautiful mulatto daughters counted their luggage. An Australian couple with a fat cranky baby sat on the ground and spooned yogurt into the baby's mouth. Three girls in school uniform darted across the green, schoolbags swinging. The conductor stuck his head in the compartment, asked to see their tickets. Alicia smiled and the man grinned back.

"A lot of men desire me," Alicia said, shrugging. Velma held her purse tight against her stomach. A tiny pulse jumped in her hip. She sipped her soda, the bottle smooth, body-shaped in her hands, until people boarded and the train lurched through Nairobi into the countryside.

Velma ate a mango, some bread and tomatoes. Alicia opened her letters. She chuckled, cooed, said, "Hmm," and laughed again. Velma felt absurd for her lack of letters. The sky darkened. Alicia dropped her fan mail, undressed, and snapped her seat into a bed. Velma snapped her seat down too but kept her skirt and blouse on. Her bra cut into her ribs. They lay in darkness, breathing out, in, until Velma slid into sleep.

She awoke during the night to Alicia shaking her.

"What is it? What's the matter?" Velma sat up. Her joints were stiff. The bed so hard. Her hip ached.

"I can't sleep," Alicia said. The sky through Velma's open window was velvet black. She strained to see Alicia's outline through the darkness.

"If I tell someone I can't sleep, " Alicia said, "for some odd reason it takes away the insomnia." She yawned, "Thanks, Vel," drew up her knees, turned and sighed into sleep.

Rage kept Velma awake till dawn. After an hour, she had to urinate, but was afraid to leave her luggage while Alicia slept, afraid to make her way into the crowded corridor to the smelly bathroom.

"Alicia," she called softly, but Alicia was deep in slumber, so she climbed onto the sink and peed down the drainhole. The act felt wonderfully defiant. She stared down at Alicia's white pile of letters. Then she climbed back onto her bench bed and stared at the wall opposite until her eyes blurred.

When Velma awoke again the sky hung light-filled and an ostrich was racing the train. Far out to field, Velma saw three giraffes nibbling at an acacia tree, and a cluster of dik-diks. Alicia awoke, gathered her scattered letters, and began to read again, as if this morning the pages would hold something new.

"My friends still can't believe I'm in Africa," Alicia said.

Velma flipped her bed back into a seat and washed her armpits at the sink, which smelled of last night's urine.

The Sun and Sand Hotel was a collection of thatch-roofed huts with a centre office and dining room. Velma felt nauseated from the rocking motion of the hot, windowless, seatless *matatu* that had carried them up-country on the bumpy road. "Most of the country's roads are unpaved," Alicia had shouted, wind blowing away words. ". . . natives travel in buses or crowded taxis. . . ." Not only had the van been full of unwashed bodies, but the other passengers carried birds or animals toward Malindi market. A frightened rooster rode the bus, wings and legs wrenched tight with twine. The twine was secured around a spoke where once there'd been a bus seat. A woman across had a hen. The hen's legs were also tied, but not her wings. Again and again the hen flopped towards the rooster and engaged in a ferocious pecking attack. Each time she drew blood. The rooster, lying on his side, could only stave her off with violent crooning sounds. During each attack, the rooster fastened bleak eyes on Velma. Neither owner paid attention. This scene reminded Velma of everyday life at Kimpese. She looked away, out the doorless back. Barebreasted women began to appear along the roadside as they moved farther up the coast. Alicia thumbed through her guide book. Never had Velma seen such variety of breasts. Banana, coconut, papaya, mango breasts.

"A person could do big business with silicon implants here," Alicia shouted. "Silicon's just sand. All that white sand on the beaches. All these breasts ripe for reshaping."

"Oh, how quaint!" Alicia warbled as she and Velma staggered around the last turn in the path. Alicia's brochure forgot to mention that the Sun and Sand Hotel was three kilometres off the main road. The driver had skidded the old van to a stop in a screech of bald tires, and no amount of Alicia's cajoling could persuade him to detour down the overgrown path to their destination. Alicia gave him a tip anyway.

"It says in the travel book they're really poor," she said. "Did you see how he stared at me?"

By the time they reached the hut (the brochure's photograph deceiving), Velma's hand was blistered from dragging her luggage, and her back pained where a shoulder strap dug. They took an outer hut. The roof smelled mouldy.

"Let's hit the beach," Alicia cried. Velma went into the bathroom and changed into her bathing suit. Her breasts were crisscrossed with red welts from the new bra.

"There are no towels," she called through the door.

"I'm gone," Alicia called. "Why don't you tell the office."

When Velma stepped from the bathroom, Alicia was indeed gone. Velma could see her already chatting with a young girl on the beach.

The office would only relinquish towels for a fee.

"I'm not asking for extras. Our room has none," Velma said.

"Perhaps you understand the need to pay then," the man behind the desk said, hand outstretched for her shillings. Velma paid for two towels.

The sand was hard and grainy. Not at all like Velma imagined sand along the Indian Ocean.

THE COCK'S EGG

"We need a deck chair, Vel," Alicia called when she saw Velma step from the office hut. "Throw me a towel." Alicia, hands stretched out behind her was watching two German men sitting on deck chairs.

Velma marched back to the office and emerged several minutes later dragging two deck chairs. Ten shillings.

"They cost extra," Velma called out to Alicia who had moved her towel and was talking, low and earnest, to the Germans.

Alicia waved. "Just go ahead and pay," she called. The chair legs scratched Velma's toes, scraped skin away.

The beach shone sugar-white. Velma dragged the two deck chairs to the water and walked the shores of the ocean for a kilometre, so blue after the amber Zaire River. She passed a woman in her midforties with a beautiful body and an ugly horseface, who knelt, giggling, surrounded by five young men playing Parchesi. "I don't give a good goddamn whose turn it is," one of the young men cried. "Molly will win." Two Kenyan men passed her, then a group of German girls.

Velma could see across the sand on her return that Alicia had her feet up on the second deck chair. Velma sat gingerly on the hot sand some distance away. Orange coral reef, blue water.

"See. What did I tell you," Alicia called, "There's even more culture up the coast. These German guys say we should take a day trip to Malindi. It's more backwoods." The German men were splashing in the water. Alicia picked up the towels, and tiptoed across the hot sand to join Velma.

Alicia slid down onto her towel, sighed dreamily, and picked the snap on her bikini top. Turned, barebreasted, to the sun. Closed her eyes. Velma looked at Alicia. Velma's large loose breasts would slip over her sides into her underarms without support. Alicia opened her eyes. "In Rome, do as the Romans do," she giggled. Velma's nipples would appear the size of Alicia's breasts. Alicia smiled and closed her eyes again.

Freckled shoulders, smooth milk stomach, fine-boned wrists. Shiny fingernails. Alicia lifted her damp hair and circled it against her hairline. Her ears stuck out. She arched her back, stretched. One leg, the other. Fine white sand clung to the blond hairs on her skin. Velma expelled a deep breath and squinted against hot Kenyan sunshine. Alicia's breasts poked at the sky. It's nice your operation caused no scarring, Velma wanted to say. But maybe small-boned women did have breasts that stood at attention. How would Velma know? Even our breasts are incompatible, Velma thought. She dug her broad back deeper in the sand. She felt anger like a tiny ocean wave lapping. Musicians, dressed in white cotton suits, stepped onto the sand, set up their instruments on the beach before the hotel veranda. The Indian Ocean shimmered a background. The men tuned their instruments and an Arabic-looking man began to sing.

When it appeared Alicia had fallen asleep, Velma rose quietly and took her towel inside. A thermos of drinking water sat on a small chunk of furniture between the beds. The water was old and warm. Velma stepped into the shower. Salt ran down her face and stung her eyes. After several minutes of lathering her sweaty body, she put out her tongue. Salt water sprayed her face. Alicia's brochure forgot to mention that the showers were hooked to the ocean. Velma stepped from its steamy centre, hotter and stickier than before, her hair stiff and unmanageable. She wrenched a clean skirt over her thighs and slapped through the quick dusk to the dining hall.

They ate fish and mangoes, rice and pineapple which slit Velma's lips like paper cuts. Velma looked at the other patrons. Their hair either hung limp and soggy with sweat, or sprang wild as if drenched in milk, then dried.

"Great Britain ruled Kenya till it became independent in 1963," Alicia read. "Since Independence, Kenyans have taken steps to emphasize their African heritage."

They ordered thick milky tea and returned to the hut together.

"Tomorrow let's grab the *matatu* up to Malindi," Alicia said. She washed in the cup of thermos water. Velma sat on the far bed.

Alicia perched on hers. It groaned and cracked and caved in at the centre. Alicia lifted the mattress. Beneath, a row of thin slats, broken.

"Oh-oh," Alicia said. "Too many mangoes. You know the office guy," Alicia said. "Do you mind calling him to fix the bed, Vel?"

The office was closed. Velma found the desk clerk on the beach with a second man, rolling dice over the packed sand. She led them to the hut.

"What problem do you have?" the man asked.

Alicia grinned. "Hi, guys."

Velma gestured to the caved-in mattress. "Our bed is broken."

The two men walked around the bed, keeping their distance as if it might attack. Considered the wreck from several angles. Spoke rapid Swahili. One said, "It is so. The bed is broken."

"We would like it fixed," said Velma.

The men looked surprised. They discussed this. "Yes," they said, "this bed must be fixed. We will send someone in the morning."

"But where will we sleep tonight?" cried Velma. All this time Alicia sat on Velma's bed painting her nails.

The men discussed some more. "Perhaps you could sleep on the floor," the office clerk said.

"Perhaps you could sleep with your friend," his partner offered. Alicia looked up from her pink nail polish and giggled.

"Fix it now," Velma said in her firmest teacher voice. The men shrugged. One fetched a hammer. They pounded three new slats into the bed frame. Stood waiting at the door.

"Heck. Let's give the poor guys a few coins, Vel," Alicia

said. She handed them coins from the wooden box between the beds. "Thanks, guys." she said. "Really."

Velma's back hurt. Her large breasts often gave her backache. She changed into her nightgown in the bathroom and crawled into stiff prickly sheets that were surely washed in ocean water.

Velma dreamed she and Alicia drove to a house in Nairobi to use the washroom. Alicia rushed in first, claiming her need was worse. When Velma sat on the toilet, she found her feet soaked from the bathroom mat, and jumped up, bladder still full. She marched outside leaving squelchy footprints, squatted, and relieved herself in darkness. Then she walked through bushes, still in her stockinged feet, to check a septic tank. Suddenly from some drain swirled up a lot of scummy water and a Harlequin.

Velma woke to a torrential rainstorm. Rain battered the soggy thatched roof of her hut. Hadn't Alicia's guidebook said no rain until October? Velma rose, peered out the window. Ripped palm branches littered the beach. The ocean swirled the shore in angry rushes. Her bra, tangled in a clothes heap on the floor, shone in the storm's light. She looked at Alicia. Alicia slept. Velma slipped off her sweat-soaked nightgown, grabbed soap and shampoo. Opened the door.

A sheet of water drove against her. She felt herself enveloped by pure, wild water. Velma tipped her head and drank. Opened her arms. Embraced the rain which slashed the earth. Chill earth beneath her feet. She scrubbed. Her soap fell in the sand. She crouched, retrieved it. Scraped soap against her skin. Rain, sand. Caught in the rough caress of wind and water. She opened her eyes to the deluge. And scrubbed. She scrubbed away Kimpese. Scrubbed away the rooster and the thief, the Malindi trip tomorrow. She scrubbed away Alicia.

"Alicia," she shouted into the storm's mouth. "I'm gone!" The storm raged on around her.

When the old *matatu,* minus its goats and chickens, limped up to the Sun and Sand Hotel, an amazed load of Kenyans stared out the missing back door at the apparition of a white naked lady scrubbing herself away in a torrential rainstorm.

"I'm gone!" shouted the wind, the storm, the whirling branches, "Alicia." The voice, triumphant, wavering, far away, "I'm gone."

Then, to this day they tell the story, toward the *matatu* filled with astonished Kenyans, streaked a lovely laughing woman through cleansing Kenyan rain. Her hair flew wild, rain slapped her bobbing breasts. A startled, defiant woman, arms uplifted. Moving. Dissolving into air.

VAMPA FALLS

There is a waterfall in Bas Zaire called Vampa. If you take the road north from Kimpese school compound, the one that climbs the hill, twists east, passes through the boys' dormitories where Mbizi died, hit by lightning as he slept in his metal bed, and follow as the road spills onto flat savannah plain, grass waving taller than a woman at the beginning of the dry season before they burn it to stubble looking for bush rats, if you continue east until the road jogs abruptly north in the middle of the plain, passing unnaturally straight beneath one flat-topped acacia tree, home to a hundred weaver birds, you will find a log bridge chiselled flat, supported by a handwire.

Cross the bridge — if it is not the rainy season and under water — and the road fades abruptly to a trail. Here, stop a moment, look back across savannah, past the lone acacia, to catch a glimpse of the brick steeple of Kimpese church, orange in late morning sunlight. Turn west and follow the stream which passes over a fallen tree being converted to coffins by the Kimpese school woodshop, one plank at a time. Pass a bamboo grove where you cut down a thumb-sized shoot and fashion yourself a flute with your two-bladed Swiss Army knife, stolen within the month by village children. The trail swings momentarily from the stream into a grove of mango trees planted long ago by Belgians, now poorly harvested, mysterious in light.

Zairians say thieves hide in this place.

If you have brought a bike, here you will leave it, for the trail now loses itself, uneven, rocky, at times dropping a metre to catch the stream bed. You hop from stone to stone, anxious the rushing water may swallow your sandal, steal it from your foot. Sidestepping, you feel the valley closing in on you. And now you crane your neck.

Vampa.

High overhead, a mere sliver of sky visible, water spills over a lip of cliff, free-falls in a thin horse's tail, crashes to the deep green pool below.

The pool where Musungu insists the merman lives.

Your clothes slide from you. You crawl the slippery rocks. Spill into sparkling cold. Swim through the crashing flooded curtain. Gaze out the prismed doorway from your forbidden cloister beneath, behind, Vampa Falls.

Everything refracts behind a sheet of perfect falling glass. You look through this curtain, north, onto a small sunbathed peninsula that juts into the pool. The only spot in this whole gorge where sunlight reaches. Catch the dissolving image of a blood-red cock, sunning himself. The scent of bird, scent of betrayal.

You swim. You swim. You climb. You stretch out naked on that hot hot rock. Filtering through your bone, your tissue. Vampa, in sunlight. Here at Vampa Falls on this hot day, nothing exists beyond the damp earth smell, sizzle of bees, a slight of shadow, wind-whiff of bougainvillea, a clutch of moths, in gusts, Vampa, Vampa, texture of time, suspended.

A DAMP WOMAN

Ko-Ko. "

White sky. Barely a sky at all. You are perspiration-soaked within your dress. You're a damp woman. And your arms, your neck, the inside of your mouth, your feet welted with water blisters. Three years here and still allergic to mangoes.

"Ko-Ko. Est-ce qu'il y a quelqu'un?"

Your legs suck the vinyl couch. You should be preparing lunch for Cynthia and Emma (the British Baptist spinsters, the three of you, on this school compound at Kimpese), it's their turn to come for lunch today, but the vendeur is here again; demands your time. A missionary can't turn him away. Already he's unveiling masks and statues from his bag. Four or five arranged on the cement outside your kitchen door. Here an ebony chess set. Here a mask. And now the Baby Jesus. The man is sparse and sharp. Keeps his eyes on his statues. Not even a quick peek at your legs. Frizzy hairs spring from his unbuttoned shirt; his head is covered in a woollen toque.

You creak the rusted screen door open and catch sight of your neighbour, Citoyen Mwanza, the biology teacher, cutting through your yard again, down to the Source. A rooster trails him, pecking at your pineapples.

"Bonjour, mademoiselle," Citoyen Mwanza calls. Bonjour. Three years you've asked him to take the path behind your house. A school compound can't function when teachers do not follow rules. He's dressed in a lined trench coat; it's humid; sweltering; thirty-six degrees.

"Que pensez-vous, mademoiselle. Peut-être vous aimez la masque."

A statement.

You let the screen door slam for Citoyen Mwanza and bend to examine the wooden masks. Your house is full of wooden masks. A boy rounds the corner of your porch. There's no such thing as privacy here at Kimpese, no such thing as an uninterrupted morning where you might sit down with a glass of grapefruit juice and plan your talk for Church Youth Ligue. The talk you have not yet been asked to give. Three years you've planned this talk. You'll speak on the tribulation of Job (his body clothed in scabs, broken and festering). A church service for youth, you started Ligue yourself three years ago. You've kept it running. The students bring their drums and their homemade guitars. They pray long prayers in French, they clap their hands to a peculiar beat. The boy now in your yard is followed by a girl; the hemp sack on her head envelops her, flops to her shoulders so she appears headless. The boy must not be more than ten (the girl, eight, seven?). Without a word, he swings his machete, thsk, thsk, thsk; he bobs and scrapes as if this were his yard. Not that you mind. It will save you hiring a boy to cut the grass. The girl staggers as her brother adds more dried grasses to her load.

"Peut-être vous aimez la crêche."

You turn back to the vendeur. He squats before you, knees pointed outward in a V. His dusty pants show the strain of squatted days before your door. But it is hard to move against this heat, so waterlogged, against the anxiety of morning prayers. You delivered prayers, six-thirty this morning (your day off) before three hundred students. You had a frog in your throat which made the students in the church aarrrg in annoyance. "Dans cette partie de sa lettre aux Ephesiens," you said, "Paul compare la lutte de la vie chrétienne à une bataille." Arrrrg. A nanny goat and two kids join the children.

"Excusez-moi," you say to the vendeur.

"Bien sûr," the vendeur sighs. His knees open slightly. *Can a woman scoop fire into her lap without her clothes being burned?* You turn sharp from his presence, wave the skinny children to your door.

"Kudia?" you ask. The little girl's legs shimmy scratches. *"Nge zola madia?"* Her brother won't make eye contact. Emma's fluent in Kikongo, Linguala too. You mime eating. *"Nge zola kudia?"* And the boy nods, speaks to his sister who crouches obediently in the tall grasses of your back yard. The females ever submissive to the males, as you strive submissiveness to God. He lifts the load from his sister's head. The children wait. You step into your dark kitchen and prepare two sardine sandwiches. The vendeur waits. All Zaire waits. Three years you've demanded the Zairian teachers appear for prayers on time. And still they laze in after Scripture reading, or not at all. No. No sandwich for the vendeur. You watch the children pull apart the slices, pick out the sardines which they lick from their fingers before they nibble down the bread.

The air fills with sudden music. "Let the waa-ter and the blood. . . ." Twelve-thirty. School's out for the day. The Ligue choir in the refectory. An English hymn. God's language. Those same religious kids (who pray long supplications at Ligue, hands uplifted) stare smirking, insolent when you teach the subjunctive in English class. *I wish I were on the other side of the world (but I am not).*

"Batete?" you asked yesterday as he slapped his flip-flops against the cement floor. "An example of the subjunctive?"

"She wish she have a husband," Batete said, and the students shrieked and slapped their palms together. In Mbanza-Ngungu two Baptist girls in their twenties are reported to have Zairian boyfriends.

"L'antilope est bien fait, n'est-ce pas?" The vendeur smooths his dark hand across the animal's grained back. You pick the smallest statue of two men carrying an upside down antelope on a pole and pay twenty-three zaires. You haven't energy to barter. Still have to ready lunch. The man packs the art slowly in his raffia sack (your fingers smell of sardines), glancing peevishly from you to the children's disappearing bread and back to you. You drag the regime of eighty-eight bananas into the entry. A gift to Emma from Kimpese's chief.

"I already received a regime of bananas from Mama Miani," she told you. "Could you use them?" (No Zairian gifts you.)

First banana bread. You whip Blue Band with the sugar, strong fast hand-strokes, and the vendeur watches under a melting sun, still as his statues, from the grass before your window, his packed bag at his feet. In the back yard the small girl staggers off under her load.

You wait the vendeur out, stare beyond him to the baobab in the elementary school yard, the narrow dusty trail down to the high school, meandering through teachers' yards and back behind itself down to the Source, where students will be washing their school uniforms, in the noisy silence of a morning Saturday. You gaze at the roof of Citoyen Mwanza's house, like you stare above your class when misbehaving students shuffle their feet, slam desks, and slump into the aisles. The porch is close with banana smell, and still you will not yield. Cynthia says, don't give them food. When you show pity, they just laugh behind your back. You slap the batter into the baking pan.

The man heaves a great sigh that lifts spare shoulders, and stoops for his raffia sack which he sets on his head. The thread in the crotch is barely holding. Live by the Spirit so as not to gratify the desires of the sinful nature. He'll turn his back on CECO compound now, head down to the village with his twenty-three zaires to buy *biteke-teke,* a calabash, or stop at Mbongombasi's for a glass of *malafu.*

"Merci, Tata," you call from the screen door, overcome with sudden shame, and he reaches out his hands. His hands are moist. So very, very moist, and sticky, like half-dried varnish. His palms move against yours, "Merci *mingi,* mademoiselle," and you feel the hard maps of his fingertips.

You're serving rabbit. Cynthia will be disgusted. Next Tuesday's her turn for lunch. She'll serve English custard. Tinned yellow powder, straight from England. You killed this rabbit. Whopped it on the head with a hammer and its eyeball popped out. You scratch your water blisters. A quarter of one. Emma may be late, she took another overnight trip to an Angolan refugee village. Won't take a day off for anything. Emma eats African, serves nothing but *saka-saka, fufu, mbika,* even mangoes for dessert. No food affects her skin. *And Satan afflicted Job with painful sores from the soles of his feet to his crown. And his wife said to him, Curse God and die.* Emma invites the village mamas in for lunch; laughs when their children pee her floor. She loves the people here. And they love her. Yes. You accept your blisters. You breathe the commingled smells of banana, onion, and peanut butter; the house hums with flat unrepentance.

When you step from the sunlit porch, head through the garden to the washline, heat swoops up from the peanut plants, pineapples, the wizening zucchini, the flattened grasses where you've tromped a path. That boy didn't work much for his food. You'll need to hire someone after all to tackle the yard with a machete. Perhaps the vendeur.

The shadow of a dog weaves in behind you, and you turn with an abrupt twist that smarts your ankle. He doesn't follow as you walk the clothesline, stripping brassieres with broken shoulder straps, faded panties, underslips and dishrags, appears too blind to follow anything. A yellow skeleton, rib cage bulging, he dogtracks the dried grasses and slowly runs into the brick enclosure of your porch. You ignore him, kneel and gather a tea towel, a green T-shirt. The dog walks backward like someone winding up to get a head start in a race. He stumbles, has trouble rising, circles the porch again, ignores the dropped crumbs, apparently uninterested in food.

"Ko-Ko." Cynthia waits before your torn screen door in a yellow V-necked dress with strong black lines. It should make her look sallow. You set the steaming rabbit stew onto the table. It's one-thirteen, who knows when Emma might show.

"She's gone Zairian," Cynthia says, and sighs. The dog's still out there, running into things through light and shadow.

Cynthia takes a dainty bite of rabbit. "I think the reason the students are so amused at you is you sing when you talk. Sometimes you have three levels in one word. Maybe you should try to spend more time with your French tapes."

You bend your head over your stew to hide a trembling anger.

"Your French teacher in England probably didn't stop you when the problem came up, as he should have done. Also you should say Jes[y], not Jes[u]. Your idea of 'sacrifice for God' was good, although I'm not sure the students understood. By the way, don't expect me at Ligue tonight. I've had religion up to here." La croix e-est a moi. Je ne peux plus jamais reculer. Alleluia. Cynthia won't dirty her hands. She runs English club. Can do that from a distance. She's annoyed at Eric, the Canadian, because he insists on helping, but speaks American. She won't allow her housegirl to touch her food for fear the girl has worms. " . . . thought of taking my class to Vampa Falls for a small fête Sunday," Cynthia says, "but now," she sighs dramatically, "it seems they are afraid of the merman. He's in there. He'll grab you, Lukalakiese says, and pull you under. Il y a les gens ont disparu, mademoiselle. I suppose there's an undertow."

"Hallo, everybody!" Emma calls through the screen door. She smells of sweat and exertion. "We just this minute climbed down the Bangu." She's puffing happily. "I didn't take time to change my clothes I haven't finished my talk for Ligue the sunrise behind the mountain was spectacular!"

"I'm sorry lunch is cold," you say. But Emma's head is bowed in a slow grace.

"We were just discussing the dangers of overinvolvement," Cynthia smiles, sticks her tongue in a tooth, (gives you a sidelong glance). There's a rumour Emma is involved with an Angolan pastor up the Bangu. Her complexion's clear; her skin shines hearty. *What is woman that You test her every moment?*

Emma's mouth is full of rabbit. She chews and nods her pleasure. "Oh," a wave of hand, a swallow, "I can't avoid it. The students have asked me to speak again at Ligue tonight."

See how Cynthia's head swivels; that small smile on her face. She's straight-backed as the steel-runged chair she sits on. The material of her dress flares bold black lines over her shoulders.

"Mvidi just now verified it down by the church as I was coming up the path," Emma says, midchew. "He said, 'On attend vos paroles ce soir, mademoiselle.' This peanut butter sauce is exquis."

"No thanks, no rabbit for me, I'll pass," Cynthia says, the stew bowl in her hands. "The military's playing war. Half the army's coming from Banana. . . " You recede into the kitchen to check the banana bread ". . . half from Mbanza-Ngungu. I might have a bit more bread. Their meeting point's Kimpese. People may be robbed or shot."

Why does it suddenly feel late afternoon? That dragging air of early afternoon uplifted. Hard energy coursing down your legs. But in your back yard peppered with orange trees and palms, the sun is overhead and in full spray. The steel table leg stings cold against your calf.

"Hand your dishes to the end," you say. "We need to clear, if Emma's to prepare her talk for Ligue."

"Thank you but I'll have seconds of stew. Perhaps the students will ask you to speak next Saturday," Emma adds compassionately. Perhaps. "I'm really not prepared. They should ask you to speak. There is no reason." Emma's knees part in relaxation. "More rabbit please. Great stew!"

Cynthia slips her chair back, crosses her legs. "A bit much seasoning. There's a woman in one of the Angolan villages who's so old the bone in her nose is no longer there. Have you seen her, Emma? Her nose goes in instead of out." Cynthia was engaged twenty-eight years ago. On her last furlough to England she ran into the man and he invited her to tea with his wife and four adult children. There were vibrations in the air, Cynthia said. You could just feel the energy. No doubt, she said, I still mean something to him.

"I'll explain to Mvidi," Emma tells you. "Yes, it's time you speak."

Dan cette partie de sa lettre aux Ephésiens, Paul compare la lutte de la vie chrétienne à une bataille. There is shadow movement outside the dining window. The dog? The statue man, poised? Waiting for your guests to leave? Your breasts rub, irritatingly, against your cotton shift. You set a plate of crusted banana bread on the table. Your eyes burn from oven heat.

"Not made with palm oil, I hope," Cynthia says.

You have the dishes cleared by three.

"I'll stop at the bastille to take a head count, make sure no girls have slipped into the bushes. We don't want pregnancies," Emma says. Then she'll prepare her talk. "You're sure that I should speak?"

Yes, you are sure.

"I've been thinking about the Twenty-third Psalm. 'The Lord is my Shepherd; I shall not want. He leadeth me beside the still waters.' Then I'm thinking of teaching them, 'Drinking at the Springs of Living Water.' Oh, I know it's an American song, Cynthia. But think of the words, 'Happy now am I, My soul is satisfied.' I'll talk of the satisfaction I derive from my work up the Bangu with the refugees." Emma is gathering her armful of long thin-rooted leaves she left on your porch, dropping small clods of earth on your cement steps. Her face is cheery with sweat. She found this new kind of leafy vegetable up the Bangu which she'll serve Monday. So you can look forward now to grass in peanut butter sauce.

"You're off? Let me walk with you, Cynthia," Emma says. Heat makes you weak and Emma strong. The two leave, shuffling dust. Once out of earshot, Cynthia will talk up Emma's adventures on the Bangu, point out your staidness, your prurience. How you struggle with the language. How morose you look these days. A knowing glance. You know, she never has adjusted. And Emma will tread on Cynthia's flip-flops and not pay attention, so cheerfully will she be drawing in the heat.

As soon as the two women disappear, you yank on your flip-flops, and march through the heat-infested breeze. Everyone sleeps. You step across a thick rope of army ants, head toward the compound's edge, insects humming in your ears, past the bastille. There all is quiet. The students still sleeping, or maybe a few have slipped into the bushes.

Already sweat pours down your face and sides, your legs move wet against each other and sting your blisters. Forty minutes to reach Vampa Falls. The thought of CECO compound shoots a pain beneath your shoulder blades, forces your clumsy gait. You've never been to Vampa Falls alone. Always with Cynthia and Emma (two Baptist spinsters to give you definition). No one's ever there. You pass the Canadian Mennonite's house, windows open to the breeze. "The creative moment," Eleanor is saying, "is intense heat." You leave the stench of drying manioc and move into the silence of a waiting afternoon, cross the low bridge, balance, cling to the wire strung on each side of the wooden walkway, scrape up the bank.

Sometimes robbers hide out at the falls. The last time a thief was caught on the compound, there was dried blood all over. Didn't they find his loot at the falls? You said, "Christ died for you," to the thief where he lay at your feet in darkness, wearing two sets of clothes, the top ones tattered. He had flashlight batteries that weren't sold in Zaire. The legal rep was running through the dark, people shouting. Perhaps you said it silently, perhaps in English, (that body thick-roped, fluid, even in stillness) for his eyes fixed blind, unmoving, on the yellow cassia. Lost opportunities. Jesus saved a thief.

The rush of water reaches your ears before you work your way into the trees and feel the spray. A refound world. The water jets, cleansed blood rushing down a wounded side. White, sparkling, its centre green. The sunlit cliffs climb, dump their water, leave it all behind. You squint, will not be pulled into their cheerful orbit. Each must bear her cross.

You're hot and smelly. Damp. You wield your way out of your sticky shift and drop your feet into the water caught below the falls. This soothes your blisters. You set your glasses on a rock. Sniff blindly at the wet clay and the cyprus. Lower yourself into the cold, cold water. Your underslip clings. Tangles. You paddle dog-like to the rock face, push out to centre. Plunge; cold grips your thighs. Caresses. And the merman slides up from below, he grabs your legs and lures you down onto his waterbed, his scaled presence bruising skin, his strength seductive like an undertow, the bottom clear and rocky. You breathe through your skin and kick your legs against that restless, teetering energy. Down your arms. Through cool, heavy thigh veins. Aching infusion. You pit all your weight against this graceful, shellacked seductor. Under your hand, the seaweed of his chest. The pool, a body that contains you. Green water fills the hollows of your bones. The throb of falls vanishes CECO compound. You climb the rock and dive again down to the bottom; dive and dive; until the clear air hurts your throat.

When at last you draw up from the water and settle on some ixora curved spongy (like a wet tongue you could sink into), you are too soon mindful of the heat and the hard ground and your chaffed sores, the impending arrival of the army, and Ligue service tonight. Your hand floats through the sound of water to touch your nose. A water beetle scurries the hibiscus, and you remember suddenly, inexplicably, the way you remember the edge of phrases or the thrum of wheels on pavement, the cold scudding rains of Manchester, England.

The afternoon sun slides down the sky, a thread of brightness strung almost to the compound. Your hair has long since dried and dampened again with sweat. You'll keep on praying. You'll hang a calendar in SS Five classroom, make the weeks slide through you. You'll buy some cloth and have a *nlele* made. A perfect green, a little brilliant, with brown seaweed crisping into pale green edges.

You move into the grapefruit grove, into the bare, caught moment between dusk and dark, see mist rising on the Bangu and, finally, CECO compound and darkened figures in the bastille doorway.

The Ligue choir is already semicircled round the drum, Emma's white face shines out among them. "Let the waa-ter and the blo-od, From thy wou-nded side which flowed. . . ." You stick to the backless bench, uncomfortably damp. The room is stifling. "Be of sin the double cure. Save from wrath, and make me pure." Your blisters rub the cloth against your skin.

Emma stands, a gentle smile. "If we could turn to the Twenty-third Psalm. The Lord is my shepherd, I shall not want."

There was a woman in the land of Uz whose name was Job; and that woman was blameless and upright, one who feared God and turned away from evil. "He leads me beside still waters. He restores my soul." *I chafe in torment and have no rest.* "Yea, though I walk through the valley of the shadow of death, I will fear no evil, for thou art with me; thy rod and thy staff, they comfort me." *What prospects has a woman that she should be patient?* "Surely goodness and mercy shall follow me all the days of my life. And I shall dwell in the house of the Lord forever." *My heart is in turmoil and is never still, and my bones burn with heat.*

From this hot room that tastes of love and pity, you can see the dark sky stretch to Vampa Falls, on to Bulungu.

Air encircles your throat like the slip of moistened palms.

THE COCK'S EGG

Citoyen Mwanza hugs his titulaire folder to his chest and hurries along the pathway to his classroom. His fingers stick together. Two hours he spent in the forest last evening retrieving glue from the frangipani tree, cutting vines open to try to catch a weaver bird. Citoyen Mwanza is hungry. The Zairian teachers have not received a paycheque in three months and his stomach groans emptily when he stands before his classes explaining the stems and nodules of perennials. He caught no weaver bird last night, his stomach is hollow, and now he has stuck-together fingers.

A dog barks by a distant fire. The British Baptist biology teacher, Mademoiselle Emma, crosses the path from her house. A moth with white half-mooned wings flutters behind her.

Last night the lights from Mademoiselle Emma's jeep washed Mwanza's window, caressed him into wakefulness and Mwanza rose from his sleeping mat and stepped through his doorway. Outside, the land was purple darkness. The heavens, hot and in motion, like a woman changing trains.

She is the kindest of the three white women here. They are so stingy, these whites, nothing gratuit. They move in a tight huddle, shop, pray, eat their evening meal together. Charge each other for their meals. They wear their rules like clothing. These British remind him of the weaver birds, weaving careful nests on neighbouring branches of one acacia tree, haughty, squabbling, fighting over food. When Citoyen Mwanza looks at Mademoiselle Emma, he thinks of food. She is the largest of the three, well-fed, she looks the best, although the village people say she eats only *fufu* and *saka-saka* at her house.

The headlights swooped backwards. He heard her laugh in darkness. They swept the football field, and whisked Mademoiselle Emma to her house at the far end of the compound. Mwanza's mouth was bitter with kola nut. The night dark as kola nut. He could hear his neighbour, Citoyen Tukeba, and some students playing Scrabble by the light of Tukeba's cooking fire. Disturbed guinea fowl clucked in the trees. The headlights died.

His dreams. Citoyen Mwanza is bothered by his dreams. He dreams of food, of Mademoiselle Emma eating: plantains, corn, groundnuts, papaya. Night after night he's forced to watch her broad arms lifting, food falling to her open lips while he, Mwanza, shadowing dream's edge, slinks like a wily snake, watching for fallen crumbs.

Last week the village rooster laid a cock's egg. Citoyen Mwanza picked it up in the dirt outside Mademoiselle Emma's door. He feared she might be watching through her thick, brown curtains so he called, *"Ko-Ko,"* and when she appeared, he extended both his palms and said, "Mademoiselle, for you," the small brown oval warm within his hands.

"Oh, what a small egg," Mademoiselle Emma said, "my hen has started laying."

"Oh, no, mademoiselle," Citoyen Mwanza said, "This is a cock's egg."

Mademoiselle Emma seemed not to understand.

"The cock's egg," Citoyen Mwanza said more loudly. "The village rooster has shown your young hen how to lay an egg.

Now you will certainly be blessed with many eggs to fill your stomach in the days to come."

Mademoiselle Emma stared at Mwanza. "Citoyen Mwanza!" she said, "that a modern young man such as yourself, tutored at the university, would continue to hold such ancient and ridiculous perceptions about the world! In the name of heaven, Citoyen Mwanza, you teach biology. What apparatus is there in a rooster that allows him to lay an egg?" Then the mademoiselle laughed. She laughed until she had to blow her nose, and Citoyen Mwanza, still holding the egg, backed off her steps.

Citoyen Mwanza nearly bumps into Mademoiselle Emma now bent over on the path, and when he trips against her she looks up and says, "Be still."

"Excusez-moi," Citoyen Mwanza says. The rudeness of these foreigners. But the woman laughs up at him and says, "No, Be Still. This flower. It's a Be Still flower. See, Citoyen Mwanza?" and Citoyen Mwanza has no choice but to kneel down beside her in the compound dirt and look into her pale hand which cups a little yellow trumpet-shaped flower with a fine leaf and a green three-segment pod. She rocks on her heels, wide and flat as a market woman's.

"I'm taking one to class this morning," Mademoiselle Emma says, "along with this," and she holds up a baobab flower, white with yellow tips, the big white petal turned almost inside out. Today she wears a red and gold *nlele* like a village woman. It loops around her heavy breasts and ties below her hip. Citoyen Mwanza needs a large wife. A wife to fetch his water, find his wood, tend a garden, pound his manioc and beans. He sleeps with high school girls, those eager to see his eraser rub out their failing mark, but they move on to prearranged marriages with men rich as their parents can afford. Citoyen Mwanza is already twenty-six years old. Losing respect. He sees this loss in his students' eyes. Yet how can he take a wife when he has no money to pay the bride price?

A noisy clutch of elementary children race up the path. Citoyen Mwanza looks at the mademoiselle, sunlight pulsing her hair, large, frivolous and silly kneeling there on the path, and he jumps quickly to his feet, not wishing to be caught in so undignified a stance.

"You do the hokey-pokey and you turn yourself about," the children sing, and do a jump-turn on the path. They carry a collection of instruments, a cowbell and a stick, beans in a jar, pebbles in a tin can, sand in a calabash, forming an orchestra as they run. Shesha-shesha shesh sh sh sh.

"And that's what it's all about!" Mademoiselle Emma sings, and greets the children with her happy laugh, as if a large white woman crouched on her hands and knees on a public path at sunrise is an everyday occurrence in an African village.

"Citoyen Mwanza, I've been teaching the small children some English songs," she says and staggers to her feet. The children swerve by, and there is stillness save for the buzzing of the flies. The heat rises and the wind dies and Citoyen Mwanza looks up at the sun, so big and round and hazy. The ancestors do not breathe. The compound smells of latrines and blossoms. He marches into the office of the titulaire for his ration of chalk.

Already before class begins, under the orange tree, the student Bilo, a surly sixth form boy with bad teeth and no understanding of biology, punches another for stealing his girl. Citoyen Mwanza has to separate the students and this makes him dishevelled and late for class. When he enters the classroom he hears the pastor's daughter complain that the fried goat meat she bought at market had a tuft of hair on it. His students can afford goat meat? A staff meeting called at ten o'clock, in the middle of Citoyen Mwanza's biology quiz, forces him to collect the papers quickly and all the students shout that therefore the test should not count. On his return, to punish them, Citoyen Mwanza orders the students to sweep the classroom with palm branches, and in their frenzy of slapping walls and desks and floor, the students stir up such a choking dust it drives them from the classroom. They run off into the bush making great shows of coughing, pretending not to hear his enraged orders to return. Mademoiselle Cynthia, the angry, scrawny British Baptist, watches from her classroom doorway, glances sharp as a machete blade. Somewhere, he hears the smush smush smush of mortar and pestle in corn. Mwanza longs to sleep through the heavy heat of his hunger pangs.

When Mwanza cuts through the grass down toward the stream to bathe in the early evening heat, he sees the bowed heads of the three British Baptist women through Mademoiselle Emma's screen door. Letters, maps, compasses. These women are always measuring their way. Mademoiselle Emma rises, then squats just inside the door, lighting a mosquito coil. Light shines through her. There is a smell in the air as old as Africa. The smell of bees in honey. A half-mooned moth floats above the mademoiselle. A tall woman with a growth on her ear runs by chasing an orange lizard. For a moment she obscures Citoyen Mwanza's view of the mademoiselle, glowing large in her bleached Matadi flour sack dress. "Minoterie de Matadi" her shoulders read in large black print. "Qualité supérieure" read the great buttocks in small blue letters. "Poids net 4536 kilos." At her hem line: "Produit de la Republic du Zaïre." The moth alights on mademoiselle's forehead. The evening light turns green and Citoyen Mwanza leaves the village compound. He passes a group of village wives, climbing back up from the stream. The right side of the road gapes in an extended hole from last night's rain, so the women come barely to Mwanza's loins as he passes. Mornings Citoyen Mwanza sees these women heading for their fields, sour mouths, backs bent beneath their hoes. They avert their eyes as Citoyen Mwanza, the teacher, passes. Afternoons these same women lean into the river, washing clothes. They scrub pants and *nleles,* flap the clothes between them. Sometimes the wet cloth descends over their heads. Then

THE COCK'S EGG

they fight their way out, laughing, their own *nleles* wet and heavy against their arching bodies.

Citoyen Mwanza sheds his clothes and sinks into the bathing hole. The water, deliciously cool and flowing, laps about his privates. The ancestors breath is on the evening wind.

Next morning at sunrise Citoyen Mwanza kneels in a patch of *ntundulu,* swallowing the citrus-tasting berries. Speak to me, oh ancestors, he prays to the morning wind. Bring me a wife. Before the students crowd into the church for morning prayers, Citoyen Mwanza heads down to the river to check the fishtraps he set overnight. Touch me with good fortune, he prays. Empty. All is quiet on the river. The wind flutters the palm trees, the sun rises like a great fire. Mwanza feels weak with vertigo. He longs for honey. Milundu compound is thick with the buzz of flies.

Saturday, after morning classes, Citoyen Mwanza walks the road to market. He stops first at the doughnut seller, caught by the delicious aroma of hot fat in the huge cast iron wok. He wanders through the market place, skirts a small boy balancing a chameleon on a stick, ignores his students, who barter for a bit of sugar in a paper cone, boiled *chikwanga* wrapped in banana leaves, a piece of salted fish, a half-glass of peanuts. He ignores the village men who gather to chew lobes of kola nut and spit their rich red juices in the market dirt, ignores the bright-eyed goats that leap sideways and butt without warning, ignores stray dogs. If he could just afford himself a small packet of *chikwanga.* A pile of fine Western shirts lies heaped at a vendeur's stall, straight from a missionary barrel. Beside them hangs a row of used tea bags. The caterpillar vendeur pours tasty green roasted caterpillars from one hand to the other; smoke blows in Mwanza's eyes.

Citoyen Mwanza is examining a stick of roasted bats when he sees the three British mademoiselles weaving their bicycles slowly down the rutted hill, shopping baskets balanced on their handlebars. Citoyen Mwanza drops the bat stick and waves. The women reach the abandoned railroad track. The two thin mademoiselles ignore his greeting. Elbows out, they steer their bikes across the ties. But Mademoiselle Emma grins, shouts, "Bonjour, Citoyen!" raises her arm, and drives her bike against the iron rail. The bike skids sideways. She tips slow motion, raised arm veering, leg lifting high. She sprawls on the railway ties, skirt billowing and caught above her knees, her glasses hanging sideways off her face. A jostle of women, market vendeurs and students close a circle round her, mocking, slapping knees, and gyrating to reinact her fall. Small children, unable to see the object of derision, run to collect stones in the hopes a crazy man is caught within their circle.

Citoyen Mwanza, frenzied, stuffs a roasted bat down the loose folds of his flour sack shirt in a desperate throw of caution to the winds. Then, seizing the opportunity, he leaps. Three manly skips and he reaches Mademoiselle Emma's side, brushes off her shoulders, offers his arm. Mademoiselle Cynthia hops off her bike like a scrawny chicken, and yanks down Emma's floating blouse. Surprised, Mademoiselle Emma smiles cheerily, flaps at her skinned knees, and puffs to her feet.

The crowd, caught in this hiatus, stares at Citoyen Mwanza who stands gallantly beside the white woman, left arm squashed against his stolen bat. "The show is over," Citoyen Mwanza says in careful English. He read that line in an American western he borrowed from the school library.

"Yes. Go on with you," the mademoiselle laughs, flinging her arms. "The market vendeurs await your business." The crowd hesitates, splinters, and streams back to the stalls.

"Thank you most kindly, Citoyen Mwanza," Mademoiselle Emma says. She extends her hand. Citoyen Mwanza takes it. Her warm fingers, mottled with dirt, curl large around his.

Citoyen Mwanza nods to the women, ignoring the frowns of mademoiselle's two friends, and strolls through the crowd, head high, past the mademoiselle's bike (ah, what he would give for such a bike), steps over the railway tracks, elbow clenching his squashed bat as tightly as one would parade a school text-book or a new bride in one's home village. His knees shake with relief. Bees moan. A half-mooned moth takes flight. Citoyen Mwanza puffs up the last muddy stretch of road and turns toward CECO compound.

By morning the news has flashed over the school com-pound. When Citoyen Mwanza breaks a twig from the lemon tree to brush his teeth, he hears the teachers' wives gossiping over their cooking fires. "Mademoiselle Emma favours Citoyen Mwanza." When he emerges from the bushes, wiping his hands on grass, he hears the students' chatter. "Citoyen Mwanza yearns for the *mundele* Emma. For her, he has performed an act of kindness." Early afternoon he hears the whispers as he strips the silky fluff from a *kapoc* tree to restuff his mattress. "Mademoiselle Emma sees in Citoyen Mwanza a husband."

Citoyen Mwanza drags home his *kapoc* fluff and lifts the cock's egg from the tin against his window. He holds the small hot egg between the fingers of his right hand and passes it over his body, head to toe. He will draw the mischievous spirit that has been causing his ill-luck into this egg. The ancestors have spoken. His fortunes include a *mundele*. Citoyen Mwanza lays the egg tenderly back in the tin, digs a small hole, breaks open the fragile shell, and disappears the black yolk into the ground. Then he lies on his sleeping mat and lusts for food.

Citoyen Mwanza, circling the hydrangea bushes at the side-walk's end, sees his wife step out of the staff room at TASOK International School. Her green Western sundress swings about her thick white legs. She shifts her schoolbooks in her haversack and wiggles her toes in her Birkenstock sandals, a habit that indicates she's satisfied. Then she heads through thick sunlight to her classroom door.

A few short years ago, Mwanza could only dream of entering TASOK school grounds, could only dream of affording a wife to fetch his water, pound his manioc and beans. Now his servants, not his wife, bake his bread, wash his trousers. Now each day Citoyen Mwanza satiates himself on tender chicken, roast cow, canned pig, pineapple pie, and chocolate bars. Now he drinks all the tea he wants, thick English tea from tea leaves Emma's mother sends. Tea golden syrupy with milk and sugar, the colour of bees and honey. The day following his marriage, Citoyen Mwanza announced to Emma that she must give away her *nleles* and dress in Western fashion. He has insisted their sons have British names. Even now he will not listen to Emma lament the boys know no Kikongo. He is a modern Kinshasa man. Emma calls him her Congo man.

" 'The Congo.' A poem by Vachel Lindsay, 1879 to 1931," Citoyen Mwanza hears his wife say through an open window. Pages rustle. "A memorial to Ray Eldred, a missionary of the Disciples of Christ, who perished while swimming a treacherous branch of the Congo." Her legs will be planted wide. Her voice will rise as she rolls into the poem.

> "Their Basic Savagery. Fat black bucks in a wine-barrel room. . . ."

Citoyen Mwanza looks at his watch. Tea break. He can hardly believe, even after three years, that he owns a watch. A Seiko. And his watch wasn't bought from a tray of watches at Kimpese market either. Why, the Kimpese market would not offer such a watch as this. Citoyen Mwanza made a list, right after his marriage, of the things he would need. One must dress, eat, live according to one's status: a penknife, a bicycle, a watch, a tape recorder,

"Pounded on the table," his wife recites in a voice shrill
   with excitement,
"Beat an empty barrel with the handle of a broom,
   Hard as they were able, Boom, boom BOOM,"

so now he listens evenings under electric lights to the tape of
Kenny Rogers bought from a Peace Corps man. This morning
he will visit his good friend Kapalata at his store. Since his marriage, Mwanza does not work at all. Emma's salary keeps them
rich. Kapalata is impressed with Mwanza's wealth. He jokes that
Mwanza should find for Kapalata a *mundele* wife also. But
Kapalata has three Zairian wives already and both men know
that he is jesting only.

"Then I heard the boom of the blood lust song
   And a thigh bone beating on a tin pan gong,"
Emma cries.

Emma never comes along to visit Kapalata who she says
stares at her; also she has heard Kapalata brag of his sexual
prowess. Such talk annoys her, she grows damp-skinned and fid-
gety in its presence.

Sometimes Citoyen Kapalata hints that Mwanza take a second young wife, but on this point *mundele* women become
difficult.

Citoyen Mwanza struts past his wife's classroom looking
neither left nor right, as befits his status.

Citoyen Mwanza laughs when he remembers Kimpese
compound. He sends fifty zaires monthly to his family. His five
young brothers attend school. Mwanza's parents have put a tin
roof on their hut. Even Emma's broad smiles on their wedding
day, which struck fear into the wedding guests, did not bring
bad luck. The ancestors surely are watching over him. Did he
not once harbour a cock's egg?

Mwanza slips the tape into the tape deck in the Kombi and pulls out onto the potholed road leading to Kapalata's cloth store.

"Mumbo-Jumbo will hoo-doo you!" chants Emma in his ears, drowning out the man's voice on the machine. It emerges lower, slower, as if his voice box is askew with emotion, ripe with silver-tongued devils.

"*Songonene!* What news?" Kapalata calls when Mwanza arrives at the store. His friend gives orders to a clerk and conducts Mwanza to his living quarters at the back where he opens two Fanta bottles filled with lime juice, and sets out *kwanga* and green mottled passion fruit.

"With life, everything is well," Citoyen Mwanza says. He leans back in his chair to gulp his juice but stops when he hears rustling behind the door adjacent, just down the hall.

"You have guests waiting perhaps?" Citoyen Mwanza says to his friend. Kapalata is becoming very stout. The favour of the ancestors surely rests on him.

No, no one, my friend," says Kapalata. He goes to his cooler and brings out a small tray of salted fish. "How is life on the great compound at TASOK International School?"

"I have no worries on that subject," Citoyen Mwanza says. "And of your own life?"

"Ah," Citoyen Kapalata sighs. "My third wife is sexually undisciplined. A woman who longs to be swallowed whole. She has conceived a fourth child before the end of the breast-feeding period of our third, and so I fear my next son will be deformed. She is too young, too active."

"Ah yes," sighs Citoyen Mwanza in sympathy, and grows restless, as if insects were burrowing beneath his skin, imagines Citoyen Kapalata's round-cheeked young wife with eyes like tiger's-eye stone, imagines Emma, fierce-eyed and sweating. Boomlay, boomlay, boomlay. BOOM.

Citoyen Kapalata sits down, and they discuss the crops, the rains, and Kapalata's recent business trip to Europe for new cloth. A light breeze stirs the palms. A bee drones in the compound.

"Citoyen Kapalata," the young clerk calls down the hall. "One needs your assistance. A young man cannot decide which cloth to buy for his wife and values your opinion."

"Always the job," Citoyen Kapalata grumbles proudly, and disappears down the hall.

Kapalata's voice fades. Citoyen Mwanza drinks more juice and eats two pieces of salted fish. Licks his salty fingers. The sound of footsteps. A closing door. Citoyen Mwanza hears wheezy breathing from the room adjacent. He eats more *kwanga*. His head grows heavy in the heat. He dreams of a field of flitting moths, of baobab blossoms, smells rich honey-bitter smells. A breathless cry springs from the room adjacent. Mwanza rises and tries the door handle.

Mwanza sees:

The top half of a woman sticking out the thick brown jaws of a snake. The huge snake gulps, is still, then spasms once again. The woman struggles, her torso wet with sweat; another cry escapes her; she breathes with difficulty. Head thrown back, her eyes are closed and moist. She shudders in the heat. Her hands rest on either side of the snake's wide jaw. Citoyen Mwanza pulls the door shut with trembling fingers. The woman is Citoyen Kapalata's youngest wife.

Fifteen minutes later Citoyen Kapalata re-enters the back room. He is jovial, sweating profusely, running his hands over his Western shirt.

"The room grows warm, my old friend," Citoyen Kapalata says. "My apologies for the delay. Me, I work always. Three wives cost time and money. What I need is a *mundele* wife like yours to do the business for me. Let us perhaps move outdoors into a small patch of shade. More refreshments?" He scratches his wide stomach and goes to the cooler for two Cokes in Fanta bottles. Citoyen Mwanza sees now on the table four fetishes: a rag, an old picture frame, three rat hairs, and a small bottle of *malafu*. He memorizes them. His throat is thick. The fetishes will give him powers. Emma will tremble at his manhood. He gulps his Coke too quickly, coughs. Citoyen Kapalata laughs, pounds him on the back. Citoyen Mwanza feels like a small lizard peering against glass. Somewhere, a long way off, a monkey screeches. They move outdoors where a light breeze softens the hard sunlight. The scent of baobab flowers and bougainvillea is strong. It mixes with the thick scent of yellow cassia. Insects buzz. Kapalata sneezes.

"I believe your wives are well?" Citoyen Mwanza whispers.

"So they are. Luvualu, are you being lazy?"

Citoyen Kapalata's youngest wife enters the courtyard with a palm frond broom. She bends and sweeps swishing patterns in the settled dust. Her hips sway with each brush. She smiles. Her throat sparkles copper in the sunlight, becomes the colour of the earth she sweeps.

"And you?" Citoyen Kapalata asks. "You have all your essential powers?"

"I am thinking, with life — which is very good —" Citoyen Mwanza says quickly, "one's fortune might always be better." He glances furtively at Citoyen Kapalata who bites into a passion fruit. Green juice squirts down his chin. Citoyen Kapalata nods.

"So I have found."

They sit in silence in the fragrant noonday heat.

Late afternoon Citoyen Mwanza climbs into his Kombi. His fingers stick with sweat. A rag, an old picture frame, three rat hairs, a vial of *malafu*. A rag, an old picture frame, three rat hairs, a vial of *malafu*. He snakes down the window and starts the engine. Boomlay boomlay boomlay boom. He slips in the Kenny Rogers tape. He's a silver-tongued devil. He's got nothing to lose. Sunlight bursts beneath Citoyen Mwanza's eyelids. He pulls onto the potted road. The tires hum. Boomlay boomlay boomlay boom. He'll lay a cock's egg for Emma. Her toes will cramp with all their wiggling. A rag, an old picture frame, three rat hairs, a vial of *malafu*. His baobab petal, he will call her. He'll be her trumpet. He'll turn her inside out. His ears fill with an orchestra of bees.

> Mumbo-Jumbo will hoo-doo you
> Mumbo-Jumbo will hoo-doo you

And Citoyen Mwanza, dizzy with lust, imagines all the Kimpese girls who lifted their skirts for him in the forest, laughing.

BROWN SUGAR

Make your own brown sugar, Lydia says. Just mix molasses with white sugar. I have some in the pantry. Help yourself. Buy local produce. Same with potatoes. They're imported from South Africa. Use yams.

Peer into Lydia's pantry. Find a sticky cardboard container of molasses. Not fit for human consumption, the container says. See a jar of coarse white sugar; beside this, three South African brown sugar bags. Full.

Wave to the sentinel at the main gate and drive the Kombi to market. You have no international driver's license. But then, who does? Speed through the intersection from three different directions. The gendarme directing traffic jumps from his pedestal, waves you over, and charges you with driving like a suspect. Gendarmes have no vehicles, and everyone knows they have no bullets in their guns. So drive away.

Swing into the market place. People shout and several gendarmes chase the Kombi on foot. They seem to be demanding money, or a change of direction. You don't understand Linguala. Horn-blowing, you skid through the market in an éclat of feathers.

At a market stall, find ten potatoes in a hollow gourd and a Matadi brown sugar bag. While you pay for your purchases, three large men grab a small boy at a nearby stall and force open his fist. A lock drops out. The large men kick. Hard thwacks. The boy thuds to the ground. His body jumps with every blow.

Next stop the Ivory Market. Trade a Seiko watch for three blue sand paintings. Barter a malachite egg down to eleven zaires. As you sit in the Kombi, window open to stifling air, waiting to pull onto the main road, a man reaches through, yanks off your necklace. The gold chain grazes. Skin burns.

Attend the volunteer's business meeting on CBZO compound. Everyone crowds into Lydia's apartment. Rabbits are first on the agenda. Item one. The up-country people say it isn't fair to have to raise rabbits for food when they're not compensated if the rabbits die. Lydia says everyone is responsible for their own rabbit venture. Item two. The up-country people want bicycles. There is no transportation to and from the villages. Lydia says she ordered bicycles two years ago from South Africa. They may arrive. Item three. Lydia says if the up-country people want to buy chocolate bars, Coke, or go out for dinner, they should pay from their personal expense account.

Leave this meeting. Step through simmering heat to the American Baptist Hostel. Climb the baobab. Grab the coiled rope of the tire swing.

Jump.

The swing free-falls six feet before the rope jerks tight. Beneath you, Diawaku, the houseboy, swats at grass with his machete, his body sleek and gleaming. Shoot by him on the upswing like a passing jet.

On your way back to the compound, buy *Time* from a street boy. Unclothed children dance about. *Mundele,* donne-moi l'argent, they call. *Mundele,* donne-moi la caisse. *Time* has a crease down the centre. It's been stolen from the post office.

Lydia drives all the volunteers to AERWA to watch Western

movies, eat hamburgers, and drink Cokes with the embassy crowd. Several rich Zairians attend wearing gold rings, gold chains. Gendarmes patrol the streets in gangs.

Seat yourself on Lydia's couch. Watch Lydia pace the apartment with her breasts exposed, the baby hanging off her arm. The flaps of her brassiere hang below her large orange nipples. Her feet make sucking noises in her flip-flops. Outside, somebody says, Someone dlopped a coconut on 'ees 'ead. Just this moment, beyond the gates, a street hawk sells a gold chain necklace for twenty-three zaires. You open *Time*. Begin to read. Breathe in the sweltering air. Feel down in your pocket the bullets from the gendarme's gun. The metal cold.

You swoop above the living room with the sudden abandon of a suspect heading one way on a Baptist swing.

While Lydia, below, stuck like molasses, puts the jerking child to her breast.

And in the shade of an African tulip tree, the sentinel will down a calabash of palm wine. And drowse.

DICTATIONS

And now he hears the munchmunchmunch. Like Saran Wrap
unwinding. Where's the bloody flashlight? Eric's fingers brush
the cool cement floor, polish circles — there — against the iron
headboard. The three British Baptist spinsters say he and
Eleanor could get electrocuted in this bed when the rainy season comes. Two years ago a student in the dormitory was killed
that way. Struck by lightning in his iron bed. And what a to-do
down in the village, the Baptist women say, deciding who made
lightning strike the boy. An arc of light swings through the
wrapped-in blackness. Eleanor barely stirs. There against the
south wall — a termite tunnel already six, eight inches high. He
can almost see it climb. There was nothing when they went to
bed. Eric heaves up from the sheets, steps, feels, swipes the tunnel. Tiny writhing grubs tumble through the glare of light onto
the floor. Eric shuffles in avoidance, glances at the bed but can
see nothing of Eleanor, relaxed in sleep. He feels for a sandal
from the closet. Munchmunchmunch. What? His fingers
enclose a second tunnel, low against the closet wall. There'll be
holes through the clothes by morning!

Eric bangs into the kitchen, the tickle of small grubs on his toes. The basin, the bleach, an old dishrag. He squashes the white grubs on the floor with his hand-held sandal. He scrubs both strips of wall, flashlight encased in the crook of his right arm, thick darkness shadowing the bobbing light. And still two brown tracks like dung trails line each wall.

Eric breathes now through a rage-constricted throat. He sprays Baygon, extinguishes the light. No moon. He waves his hand before his face. Not even outlined. Eleanor's breathing barely audible across the room.

※◇※◇※

Late morning, Eric throws the bleach water onto the hard packed courtyard dirt. Emmanuel stoops before the doorway, pounding *fufu* with mortar and pestle.

"*Kiambote,* Monsieur Rider."

"Bonjour, Tata. Comment va le chien?"

Emmanuel works in the kitchen fixing fried eggplant and beans. Eric's stomach is queasy still from yesterday's English class.

"Good morning, class."

Sssssssssss. He stands in the doorway, blinking dimness. Seven-thirty. Hot sunlight shines through limba leaves and dapples the worn blackboard — there'll be a glare. "On ne peut rien voir, monsieur," Masakusu will say.

Class STA Three rises (Kifudi with deliberate slowness?). They look at him intently, smiling, mouths closed so he can't tell from which teeth the hissing issues. The wind lightly whisks the *limba* tree and leaves rub the wall. A few chickens flap and squawk, and scratch before the open door.

"Good morning, class."

"Good moning, Meesta Rider."

"You may be seated."

"Sss."

They love nothing more, the Baptist spinsters tell him, than watching a white teacher lose control. Eric feels it is essential he stay calm, rehearse for something more, some bigger part. Should he say, "If you choose to continue this — sound — I will leave and you can find another English teacher"? A swirling in the *limba* tree. Or is there no sound at all?

Emmanuel sets the eggplant on the table. Sliced paper thin. He wears Eric's Western T-shirt like a badge, pond-rippled over his protruding stomach. Eleanor appears across the compound, stepping from her physics classroom, small and sure, surrounded by a clump of eager girls. Emmanuel nods, grins at the window.

"Madame vient." He scuffs into the kitchen for the beans. Eleanor moves reassuringly against that scorched white sunshine.

"Hi, Eric. Good day? Bonjour, Emmanuel. Que ça sent bon!"

Ssssssssssssss. The eggplant slivers are sizzling hot.

Afternoons, after Emmanuel goes home, after siesta, Eric and Eleanor take their books into the sun-streaked humidity and wait for students. To live like this . . . says Eleanor and sighs luxuriously. Sometimes a long-stretched frightening blank skims over Eric, holds him in its core. Unfocused image teetering into possibility. Then gone.

Often, instead of planning next day's English class from his *English for Africa* guide: "Buying Some Groundnuts," "Up a Tree," "A Story: Who Killed Our Teacher?" Eric reads Reader's Digest Condensed books. He rides familiar story lines, clings to clichés, peels back the green-brown pictures to step against the outline of an elm tree by a brook. The tree trunk finely cracked, as tree bark at home would be, not large and looming like the baobabs. A rough, bowlegged cowboy hand-scoops water from the pasture stream. Eric closes his eyes and tastes the cold spring water on his tongue: their water barrel here is covered with fine mesh to catch mosquito larvae. He sniffs the flutter of musty page, transforms those fragile, brittle leaves to cool prairie air, while Eleanor frowns into her physics books; her yellow pages bend in yellow light.

He turns to his dictations. 1. Don't push me. 2. My husband wants his supper. 3. Do you want an American song first, or an African one? 4. It's very expensive, you know, and I've got three wives and a lot of children. He must remember to hand the papers back with his right hand. It feels so awkward. In Zaire, the British Baptists say, the left hand is used to wipe oneself.

". . . when a pot of cold water is placed on a hot burner," Eleanor is explaining. "Hmm, oh — well — on a wood fire, say, the temperature of the water increases. The heat flows from the hot fire to the cold water. . . ."

"Monsieur." Standing shy. Legs planted wide, collarbone shining. The insolence of class forgotten. "I need help." He didn't remember to watch for them, this clump of girls, moving in shuffling rhythm from the dormitory like a self-imposed shield of body guards. Eric is trustworthy because his wife is here. And still the girls protect themselves with numbers. Ten minutes alone in a teacher's house and a girl is expelled from school. Sent back to the village with her head shaved. Really, they want nothing more than to get into a white man's good books, the Baptist spinsters say, or frankly, in his bed, in hopes he'll sail them off to England. They blink. Or Canada. Lands of milk and honey, Eleanor laughs.

But look how the girls turn to Eleanor. The awestruck faces, the bright bright eyes. They breathe in her freckled throat, her narrow blue-jeaned hips, those oversized red glasses.

The British Baptist spinsters have grim stories of white women who take Zairian husbands. One went blind, was left to sit all day with small children and the mother-in-law in a cramped courtyard in Kinshasa while the husband went philandering. Philandering? No money to return to England, not even to buy stamps. A third world myth, Eleanor says after.

"What is it?"

"We can eat pounded yam and pepper soup een the dining hall. Monsieur, what ees the question?" Eric prods and drags out and corrects. "Not what *we can* eat, Mpinga. What *can* we eat in the dining hall?"

Look how they stalk Eleanor and giggle. Eleanor, curled up on a canvas chair, all sunlight gathered into her, and barefoot too, ". . . is a type of antennae used for the detection and broadcast of television waves," she tells Masakusu. She rolls her eyes at Eric as Masakusu nods.

"I — been — yet. How I make the question, monsieur?" Mpinga's body close to his. Hair clenched-stiff palm tree braids that almost crackle. Sweat and palm oil.

"Look at page forty. When the source of sound travels away from the observer, the pitch is lower. For example, read here, the pitch of a siren on a speeding fire truck drops abruptly as it passes you. Damn, this book is useless in Zaire!"

"Don't try to form a question, Mpinga. I have not been there yet. . . ."

Eric teeters on the edge of memory while Diadia lays aside her scribbler and strokes Eleanor's hair into fine-braided loops, and the girls cluster in and watch. *Cruel comme la memoir.* Where did he read that?

Boys from SS Five, grade eleven, have wandered over on the pretense of needing to use the library. Eric is librarian and guards the thirty-odd English books under lock and key. The boys now are seated on the low wall around their patio. The air, so hot and wet, makes breathing difficult.

How many children you have, monsieur?

None, Bakwa, Madame Rider and I have no children.

How many children you have in Canada, monsieur?

We have no children, Museka.

None, nowhere, monsieur?

None, anywhere, Museka.

Furtive smiles widen to contemptuous grins.

"We want to wait, Bakwa," Eleanor leans over a student's scribbler, smile warm, her cream throat glistening, face oval-shaped against her braids. Eric's never seen her hair like this. The students' eyes are caught by her eyes as she lays herself before them, bare and reaching. "We don't want children now. I want to work. Maybe later, maybe not. We'll decide when we go back to Canada. In Canada women want equality."

Silence. "Decide, madame?" and then a roar of laughter.

Eleanor fingers the soft limp braids which breaks the girls into small laughter, and her face rounds with pleasure.

The wash of yellow light floats into a fast darkness, and Eric moves indoors to light the lamp and reheat leftover beans. The eggplant slices they eat cold. Eric meant to suggest an evening walk — just he and Eleanor. The students stayed too late. Strange land of silhouettes. Eleanor bites an eggplant slice, leans into the lamp, her winged hair reflecting fire. Outside a cool breeze stirs the black and velvet air. Their guinea fowl flutter in the trees; croak and settle. Fruit bats swoop the rabbit hutch and in the forest beyond the compound, a nightjar sings.

It isn't until Saturday afternoon they ride their bikes down the steep hill from the compound before the climb to CINAT, bathing suits tucked inside their shorts. Eleanor drops away from him, floats down. She sings, her voice unwinding like thread behind the breeze. Eric catches huffs and clumps of words. "Huh, huh twilight hmm hmm prairie, Where the pale blue mm mu hide . . . da da da da da da da just to have you by my side, In dreams huh huh huh smiling. . . ."

What puts this song inside her ribs, exuding melody, as Eric strains, blinks sweat, and tastes the bittersweetness of an afternoon's retreat?

His weight pulls him ahead on the descent. He passes a group of women, heads piled high with firewood. They stand backed to the tall grasses by the road, faces turned up to receive him. *"Mbote, Mamas."*

"Da Da twilight on the prairie I'll be dreaming woo hoo hoo. . . ." He hears the metal grating stones. When he turns she is already sprawled, the women enclosing her in their tight semicircle, while Eric skids to a trembling stop and hefts back up the hill. Eleanor's knees are skinned. Her palms shed gravel.

"I won't be a minute, Eric," she calls, and before Eric can reach her on the incline, she swings a bleeding knee over the bike and sails away.

"What happened?" Eric calls, neck craned in fright. A scraped hand flaps dismissively in air. "I should have realized, Eric. The British — Cynthia warned me. . . ." Her voice weaves back. " . . . my legs? I'm wearing shorts!" There's grit in Eric's ears and nose. The women have disappeared. He can see their loads of sticks travelling bodiless through high grasses. Eric retrieves his bike from the scorched sand and lumbers after Eleanor, past a shelf of dried palm nuts heaped like dust beside the road.

"Cinq zaires," the man in the ticket booth says. The Swedish doctor's teenage children, home for congé, do lengths in the pool. Eleanor drops her shorts. Beneath, a peach bikini. Her knees glitter bloody in the sunshine. The children stare.

Between her small breasts is a ring that brings together the cloth over each breast. Eric wants to hook his fingers in and guide her close. He wants to feel her gentle heat flow to his bones. To weep into her drooping cheerful braids. She sees him watching, smiles, "Shall we?" and her brown shoulders ease into the water. Eric doesn't want to enter yet. He drops down at the pool's edge and watches her brown legs flow through grey-blue, her swimming effortless and smooth. He's brought a book along. *Household Stories by the Brothers Grimm, 1886.* He found it in the pantry. Perhaps he'll place this one in his library collection. He's sent a memo to Kinshasa that he hopes to increase the library's stock to fifty books by Christmas.

"The Death of the Hen." Eleanor's joined the doctor's teenagers. Once upon a time the cock and the hen went to the nut mountain. Eric looks across the valley to the Bangu, rolling in cloudless sunlight. The British Baptist women say the rains will start within the week. And they agreed beforehand that whichever of them should find a nut was to divide it with the other. Now the hen found a great big nut — Eleanor's feet plunge upward from the still grey surface, ankles streaming water, her skin has darkened incredibly in two short months — but said nothing about it and was going to eat it all alone, but the kernel was such a fat one that she could not swallow it down, and it stuck in her throat so that she was afraid she should choke.

Cock, cried she, run as fast as you can and fetch me some water or I shall choke.

So the cock ran as fast as he could to the brook, and said, Brook, give me some water, the hen is up yonder choking with a big nut stuck in her throat. The water shimmers, flat, sheeted glass. Eric's heart pounds his rib cage. Where? But she's behind him dripping the cement and talking to the doctor's daughter. The girl's breasts are larger than Eleanor's. She's taller too. The girl is looking down at Eleanor, they're laughing, something about the French teacher at the international school in Kinshasa.

So then the cock brought the water to the hen, but, alas, it was too late; the hen had choked in the meanwhile and lay there dead.

The Peace Corps man in Molembe told Eleanor and Eric on his last trek out that a village woman found a dead chicken on her doorstep. A curse put on her by someone in the village. And within the week, she died.

"Fascinating!" said Eleanor, and sucked juice from her orange slice. The juice ran down her fingers, the colour of the dripping bathing suit that she now wears.

The sun heat strokes the small of Eric's back. He doesn't want to leave this small oasis. Everywhere he hears English. Eleanor's French has improved dramatically in the last month. Except with Emmanuel, and idle chitchat with the teachers, Eric rarely uses French.

As it turns out, many animals: mice, a fox, a wolf, a bear, a stag, a lion, grieve for the dead hen, even lie down across the stream so the wagon carrying her dead body can pass over. The cock draws the wagon with the dead hen safely to the other side, but when he returns for the mourners, the animals some- how all tumble into the water, the story gives no reason for it, one on top of another, and are drowned. So the cock, left all alone with his dead hen, digs her a grave, raises a mound over it, and laments until he dies. And so they are all dead together. The air feels chilled. The rains? Eric slips into the sunwarmed pool and does six lengths.

It is seven o'clock, but light under a slivered moon when they leave CINAT and head for CECO compound. An almost cool breeze fans their faces. They ride past ant hills and cattle grazing, an old abandoned restaurant, its mud bricks crumbling, impermanent.

"I think next summer we should travel in Kenya," Eleanor says.

"How are your knees?" It's the closest Eric can bring himself to speak of the incident, this hostility that flaps his heart against his chest.

Eleanor looks surprised. "Oh, fine. Say, Eric. Citoyen Mwanza talked to me today about a village trip. We could leave next Saturday, after my class, be gone by two. It's up the Bangu. We'd stay overnight," Eric looks to the Bangu, someone has built a small brush fire, flames leap and pounce, "and climb back Sunday afternoon. There's Angolan refugees up there. A whole village of them! They'd be honoured to have us, Mwanza says."

"Did you hear that Citoyen Willa-Willa's nephew stole Willa-Willa's things and fled back to his village?" They have passed into the forest. Rats scuttle in the grasses. "Willa-Willa was paying for the boy's schooling! Letting him live in his house!"

"Yes, he told me."

The teachers talk to Eleanor as if she were a man.

"He took his tape recorder!"

Eleanor disappears into a bar of dark and out again; her arms shimmer in the dim moonlight, her legs skim circles. She seems not to touch the ground. Eric feels he will see her always like this. His memory will hold her in these strange braids, levitated, glistening past palms trees on a moonlit night, sharp scent of magnolia, the salted texture of her skin, her pores, soaking in Africa. Air moves past Eric's ears in a soft sssssssss.

And now voices, water splashing.

"The British Baptist women have told the students I speak vulgar English." Eric feels he has to say this, hook her to reality. His voice comes out petulant. "You know, tomato, tomawto, collect the papers, don't take them in." Eleanor's smiling at the moon, her cheekbones thin and silver.

They near the log bridge and the final climb to CECO compound. The path beneath his bike is strewn with shadows of ancient wood. If he could only hold her from the edge, evoke the old familiar stretch of measured time. They reach the Source. He skids his foot in gravel and reaches out to brush her into pause, so he can take her bike across the log. But when he looks up he sees naked village girls in panties scrambling up the bank. Water clings to breasts and thighs, shines like blisters in the moonlight.

"Come on, Eleanor!" Eric grabs her bike and trots the thickest log, rolling the bike along the parallel log, cracked and dipping in the middle. "Eleanor, I'll be right back. I'll come for you."

He's scuttling back. The girls don't look his way. She is surrounded. Hands slide over her breasts, her arms, her hips, her soft brown braids. Eric runs across the log now with his bike. Her hair in wisps; a bougainvillea blossom. She stands so still, turns her small form within their hands. Receives their touch. A webbed cloud skims the almond moon, her white shape darkens, and the young girls pale. She reaches out her hands, touches them back, until her body slips undefined and dissolves into theirs. When Eric thunders back across the log and stands, arrested, separate, she smiles, eyes clear as porcelain. She lifts the hands from her body, and the sky opens to her as she steps across the log. The water twinkles inky, reflecting littered stars beneath her feet. A nightjar flutters on the road in sudden moonlight, then swings into the colocassia. The *nzenzi* sing.

Riding the half mile back to CECO compound, Eric jumps when Pastor Ntondo slips from the darkness on the road down to the spring.

"Masa!" the pastor calls, feet sifting sand. *"Masa! Masa!"* and the young girls run into the forest to hide their legs until he passes.

Eleanor begins to sing, nnnnnnnn nnnnn nn nnnnnnn, a melody without words, like Zamfir's flute. The scent of wet earth and oleander strengthens. Her bike wheels murmurmurmurmurmur against the darkness, disguising Eric's choked and anguished breathing.

HIPPO

Fioti was scrubbing clothes on the shores of the Kwilu the day the hippo bit Izzie Rosehill in half. They say her strange black *mundele* body came floating down the river stuffed in an inner tube. Fioti let Dr. Schappert's shirt float away. They say he splashed into the water, sank to a swim, caught hold of the tube which circled in the gentle current and towed it in. The body was Isabelle Rosehill, the black American Peace Corps woman who arrived last month in Vanga. Much of the intestines and guts had been washed away, the body held together by skin and muscle on the right side.

They say Fioti ran up the path and met Mama Schappert coming down. His voice choked silent, he just grabbed and pulled her through the star grass and napier to the shore.

They say Mama Schappert dug her nails so hard into his flesh, his arm turned white. She said, Where are the rest of them? Where is Melissa? Where is my husband?

Fioti left the laundry piled on a rock, drew in a pirogue and Mama Schappert crawled over the side, slipping in the muck and banging her shins. Fioti paddled upstream. Mama Schappert rode erect, her hand stuffed in her mouth.

Even eight-year-old Melissa knew to lie still and not yell when the hippo surfaced. He surfaced in the middle of the party floating downstream on the Kwilu. His great brown streaming back materialized, Dr. Schappert said, and he rested a moment like a giant stone. The breeze shivered the leaves of the leguminous trees that formed the shoreline and dipped low in the water. A bird of paradise sang a sharp note. Then Izzie Rosehill screamed. Dr. Schappert said she screamed and flailed and crashed herself right out of her inner tube. The hippo went down and surfaced again, shaking his head and snorting. He fixed his small eyes on the shrieking Izzie Rosehill, yawned open his jaws, and bit her through.

Dr. Schappert remembered the bird of paradise, he said. How its call trilled, sharp and repetitive. The hippo went down and the body came up, organs swimming away before the rest of her. Dr. Schappert caught the body and stuffed it in the inner tube, and everyone moved to get the children out of the water.

The hippo surfaced again. There was no shoreline, only elephant grass and branches to snatch at. Brown jaws yawned wide. The hippo caught Melissa Schappert by the foot and pulled her down. Dr. Schappert grabbed the child's hand and went along, beating the hippo, slow motion, about the eyes and nostrils with his fists and feet. The others scrambled up the branches.

Three times they surfaced. Hippo. Child. Man. Clinging together like a grass chain necklace. The hippo, left nostril oozing blood, released his hold and slid down without them. Dr. Schappert rammed Melissa into an overhanging branch and scaled it himself. It was like being flushed down the toilet three times, Melissa said. Her foot was bitten through, but not off. Now began the long wait in the trees.

Melissa cried, low drawn-out wheezes, and Dr. Schappert

THE COCK'S EGG

cried too and began to sing, "It's cheese, cheese, cheese that makes the world go round. . . ," and everybody joined in.

Fioti and Mama Schappert reached the spot two hours later drawn by voices, singing, "Merrily, merrily, merrily, merrily, life is but a dream" in a round. The seven climbed down from the trees and rode back to Vanga where the villagers ringed the body remains in eerie silence. They say the village albino watched from a distance behind a baobab. Dr. Schappert jumped from the pirogue in thigh-deep water, Melissa in his arms, and ran through the scattering of goats and chickens up the pathway to the hospital. The village rooster sailed behind him all the way. Fioti beached the pirogue and led a straight-backed Mama Schappert past the silent villagers up to the house, his arms heaped high with unwashed laundry.

What to do with a black *mundele* body. The wife of the Mission Aviation Fellowship pilot worked the radio until late afternoon, in contact with the American Consulate in Kinshasa. Will the family in North Dakota want the remains? Shall we bury her here? The body was decomposing. The temperature forty-two degrees. The weekend had begun in North Dakota; the family could not be reached.

Discussion moved to Dr. Schappert's house. The Zairians held their own council in Tata Kunda's tin-roofed hut. Fioti was chosen to stand guard over the body and fight off the village dogs. By midnight the whites had reached a decision. Now how to get the body to Kinshasa? Whites flying a black body, bitten in half, into an international airport to be picked up by more whites was not wise. There'd be questions, bribe demands, a city court.

At two in the morning Dr. Schappert and Fioti loaded the body onto the back of the construction truck and began the long twelve-hour drive into Kinshasa. Dr. Schappert pulled out of Vanga past palm trees standing like construction paper silhouettes, past Tata Kunda's hut, his tin roof gleaming. Fruit bats swooped the headlights. The Kwilu washed silent.

Saturday morning the plaintive cry of mourning doves disturbed the village. A child dreamed of hippos lunging against water. The sentinel found a snake in his hut, its fangs sunk deep in a live frog. A village woman making sesame butter slivered herself, sliding the pounding board between her thighs.

Sunday morning the truck returned. Sunday evening the missionaries held a memorial service in Vanga.

We are gathered together, the pastor began. At this moment Zairians filed in, filled up the backless pews. The women, wailing, perched on the window sills. Small goats perched there too. The missionaries craned their necks from the front rows.

. . . to mourn the tragic and untimely. . . .

Ndoki! Tata Kunda rose. Council has met. Who turned into a hippo and ate the black *mundele* woman from America? The ancestors have spoken. Dr. Schappert is named.

Imagine.

We are gathered together. . . , the pastor faltered.

"Lu zinzodolo lutala," the Zairians sang. Dr. Schappert bowed his head against his hands, thin shoulders sagging. Fioti sat beside his employer on the hard church pew, his great brown back resting, still as a stone.

▰◣◸▰◣◸▰

Toward midnight, Fioti, eyes throbbing, massive head jerking against the pain in his bruised nostrils, the taste of *mundele* in his throat, lumbered down the river bank and slipped into the Kwilu's healing waters, opened wide his jaws and sank beneath the surface where he rested, snorting, blowing pink bubbles, twirling his ears, until dawn touched the sky and his fellow villagers led Dr. Schappert away.

Then Fioti surfaced, shook off the water, the *ndoki,* and strolled up the hill to prepare breakfast for the doctor's family.

GAMING

Bernard writes his initials in black felt pen on the mangoes and grapefruit growing outside his door. *B.E.* Otherwise the Zairian kids steal them while he sleeps, black shadows sliding through a blacker night, and sell them back to him the next day. Bernard is without househelp. Mazwika's mother died last week, so Bernard allowed him two days off to attend the funeral. He offered five zaires to help pay for the burial. This week she died again. Mazwika acted out her death: diarrhea, vomiting, dropping to the floor in a heap. Bernard let him go, but he was damned if he'd give Mazwika five more zaires. Mazwika glides around with his stripped palm frond broom, bakes hard bread, sweeps the compound while the dirty dishes wait, and steals sugar when Bernard is at the hospital. And he watches Bernard without looking, just as Dr. Schappert's wife does, when Kimberly comes to stay.

Kimberly watches Bernard initial fruit. He squints into the mango tree and Zaire's white light hurts his eyes.

"Let me do some, Uncle Bernie!" Kimberly calls. And Bernard smiles, and lifts the child by her sunlit thighs into the dappled mango leaves to reach the high ones.

At nine o'clock Bernard makes a double bed on the floor, strips down to his undershorts and crawls in beside the child, her parents asleep sixty miles away at Moliambu. At ten o'clock the generator cuts. The lights extinguish. Bernard moves his fingers across the child's hip in time to her gentle breathing.

⬥⬥⬥

Mazwika enters his employer's house in dawn's grey light, brushing his teeth with a twig. A small snake sleeps in the kitchen, coiled around the doctor's bicycle wheel. Mazwika cracks its head, ties it head to tail and buries it in the backyard to protect against evil.

Mazwika grew up in love with the smell of the whites. Petrol and Baygon, denim and tea, perfumed soap, slick sweat and a dried-corn-husk staleness. The whites set foot outside only to flee snakes or to hop on their bicycles and visit their white friends.

Dr. Bernard is still asleep. He is not in his single bed, but on the living room floor, his arm around the missionary child from Moliambu. The child lies on her stomach, nightdress up, her underpants revealed. Dr. Bernard sleeps on his side, his hand in the small of the child's back, his fingernails clear, the texture of onion skin.

⬥⬥⬥

In the morning Bernard plays tapes. The music twists down the clay path winding to the river. "The Congo's my haven, for frolic and bathin.' " The sun, a startling presence, tips the dry grasses outside their door. Kimberly crawls out of bed.

"Can I pick some leading lady for the breakfast table?" she asks.

"How's *my* little leading lady?" Bernard teases. He undoes the button on her nightgown and slips it up her body, cuts bread and pineapple in the kitchen, singing, "The angels beckon me from heaven's open door, And I can't feel at home in this world anymore," while Kimberly pulls on her clothes and runs to the back yard to cut three leading lady hibiscus blossoms.

Mazwika unscrews the gas bomb tap, and holds a match to the burner, which leaps to life. The doctor dislikes him in the kitchen but he must make morning tea because the doctor has a guest. Mazwika steps into the compound and picks a pineapple and two grapefruit. He looks up into the branches of the grapefruit tree and sees *B.E. B.E. B.E. B.E.* A bird of paradise trills in the forest. The ground is thistle-strewn, sunny with dust.

When Mazwika returns, the doctor slips into the bathroom. Mazwika hears him brushing his teeth and spitting at the sink.

"Mbote, Mazwika. We don't want waste," the doctor says. This doctor only uses the gas oven for bread, which he bakes himself. The doctor slips around Mazwika and turns off the gas burner. He steps on a stool to reach the bread. When the doctor and Mazwika stand side by side they measure the same height. But Mazwika feels taller. Mazwika halves the grapefruit. His palms stain grey from the black felt of the doctor's initials. The child wakes and stumbles outside to pick hibiscus flowers. The doctor draws her on his lap and whispers, "My chick-pea, my leading lady," brushing her hair off her face. When he begins to nestle the strands into a braid, Mazwika heads outside to scrub yams for lunch.

"Why did the fly fly?" Mazwika hears the doctor say through the screen.

"Because the spider spider."

Mazwika decides he shall ask Simbi Mayamona for further English lessons.

※▲▽▲▽▲※

At breakfast the kitchen air glazes sticky with flower scent. A hospital worker knocks on Bernard's door.

"Mama Kiamfu will have her baby now."

"I need to leave you, chick-pea," Bernard says. "When I come back we'll go swimming." Kimberly smiles up at him, lips shiny with pineapple juice.

Mama Kiamfu, child-sized, will need a caesarean. When Bernard sticks his head in the operating room, he sees Mama Kiamfu sitting straight-backed on the operating table, thin legs dangling in a triangle of light, a large needle stuck into the base of her spine. Nurse Simbi has begun preparations, has laid out the towels, has set the bucket at the base of the operating table, and turned on the fan.

While the medication takes effect, Bernard slides into his gown and mask and scrubs up. He places the soap and brush on the metal cupboard, pours water into the bowl and sets the timer for seven minutes. Bernard scrubs his palms, between each finger, his knuckles, the tufts of hair below his knuckles stiff like palm fronds, up his wrists, thickly soaped, around his arms, the knuckles again, the palms, and last the fingernails. The wire brush leaves his skin red, almost burned. Puffs of soap suds fall on Bernard's feet, sticking his toes together in his flip-flops, soap plops onto the cement floor, shining, and in the adjoining room Mama Kiamfu lies waiting, eyes bright with child-trust, a blanket rising upward from her waist.

Mazwika's father was a houseboy to missionaries from Lethbridge, Canada. As a child Mazwika hovered, hidden behind a mango or *lifaki* tree, in the yard where his father was employed. He watched the children of his father's boss, wild white comets with flying feet and elbows. The children scratched lines in the compound dirt and hopped about their drawings. They threw a ball, ran hard, and knocked each other to the ground, a game composed of illogical rules. They brought playthings out into the sun-sharp compound and concentrated for hours in studied play. Sometimes they tired of a toy and left it to rust or decay in the yard, pummelled by rains until, feigning indifference, Mazwika would venture from his mango or *lifaki* tree, poke timidly at the rusted tractor, or wheelless doll pram. Sometimes the girl would whirl on him a stare so fierce he'd skulk trembling from the yard. Other times she'd laugh, pale hair stuck to her face, and offer him the discarded object, "Dja want it? Take it." By the time Mazwika turned sixteen, he had a Barbi doll, three fire trucks, a tin lizzy, a spinning top, a broken set of tin dishes, and a miniature broom. This stash he kept beside his sleeping mat between himself and his four younger brothers in the sleeping room of their two-roomed hut. After his brothers, one by one, fell into a whistling, snoring dreamworld, Mazwika would lie awake and watch his metal collection shimmer in caught moonlight. When Mazwika turned nineteen and finished sixth form at school, his father arranged for him a job on Vanga compound. A missionary doctor's house. A man without a wife. This will be easy, Mazwika's father said. It is the women who are hard to please.

THE COCK'S EGG

Bernard cuts into skin which draws away like a slit mango. "Oh Lord, you know," he sings, "I got no friend like you." He checks the lining of Mama Kiamfu's uterus. "If heaven's not my home, then Lord what will I do?" Mama's hands lie relaxed at her sides. Nurse Simbi hovers, so Bernard tells her to pick up the towels. He peeps over the blanket that protects Mama's eyes from the happenings below her waist, and those eyes regard him calm, unblinking. His hand pushes against Mama's appendix, and he lifts the baby out while Mama contemplates the ceiling beyond her cloth wall. The baby is slippery, chalky white, and hardly cries. Mama reaches her arms and draws the baby to her spent breast. They lie still together while Bernard sews Mama up.

Bernard visits a patient with bilharzia and carries to the lab a sample of bloody urine. "When the shadows gather round my door, I'll fly away," he sings. He checks the vital signs on a small boy with kwashiorkor. A dead body is brought in from Songo, nose and ears stuffed to keep the bugs out and the spirit in. Bernard turns the body over to Nurse Simbi.

Bernard scrubs up again in the hushed morning heat, steps over a grumbling rooster to smile in at Mama and pat the baby. "Help the baby onto the nipple," he calls to Nurse Simbi. "Scrub the birthing bed with Lysol and see that Mama has movement in her legs," and then he dances home to Kimberly. The sun is a dark bruise in the sky. She waits in her bathing suit, all red and shiny with a diagonal blue and silver stripe across the bodice.

"Not it!" Kimberly cries when she sees him coming. Bernard growls and chases her and Kimberly runs, shrieking, down the river path. Bernard stumbles over ground roots, and Kimberly, choking with laughter, evades his grasp until he catches her by the waist and they sprawl together in the soft dirt. Kimberly wiggles from his grasp and darts among the trees, but Bernard calls, "Let's go for a dip in the Kwilu, chick-pea! Calling my leading lady!"

Bernard and Kimberly dive and splash and play leapfrog. When Kimberly tires, they float. Her hair streams behind her like aquatic grasses. When she stands, Bernard slips his arms around her from behind and hugs. He holds her like that a long time. The sunlight is fierce through the *musa* and ferns.

On the kitchen cupboard, Mazwika finds a block of cheese and a sack of onions. The doctor's hair is wet and sticky from his swim. He peers into the freezer, shakes his container of flour.

"Freeze the cheese," the doctor says.

Mazwika places the onions in the refrigerator, cuts the cheese into four small blocks and wraps each section with the doctor's crinkly paper. The cheese smells terrible and the smell clings to Mazwika's hands.

The doctor stares into his frozen flour.

"How's my tapioca flour?" the doctor says. He bumps the container on the counter, stirs the flour with a knife. "These beggars won't give up, Mazwika," the doctor says.

Mazwika centres the last piece of cheese on the crinkly paper and carries the four blocks to the freezer. The doctor's knife slides through the flour and in a dozen places the flour humps and writhes.

"I should send you to Canada," the doctor says to the worms. "Thirty below. That'd teach you to play games with me. Come on. Die."

Mazwika picks the lye soap from the kitchen counter and scrubs and scrubs the cheese smell from his fingers.

　　　　　　　　THE COCK'S EGG

Bernard and Kimberly lunch on eggplant, *fufu* and papaya. Kimberly asks to look at the painted gourd hanging on Uncle Bernie's kitchen wall. It is stained sky blue. Jagged mountain motifs scratch the surface.

"What's it for?" she asks.

"Zairians use gourds for dispensing water or receiving alms," Bernard says. "But mine's a decoration, Kimie. Mine's for play." Kimberly spins the gourd on the table. Its base is uneven and the gourd falls on its side. Bernard and Kimberly lie down on the double bed in the living room for an hour siesta. They play Button-de Button-de Be So High until Kimberly drowses.

▨◆▽◆▽◆▨

Mazwika drags the doctor's ironing board to the front porch and sets the charcoal iron on the fire to heat. The doctor insists Mazwika iron everything. Worms. The doctor has a fear of worms. Mazwika irons the sheets, the towels, the doctor's underwear.

"When you hang my clothes on the line to dry," the doctor says, "a parasite lays eggs in the wet heat. The eggs hatch worms that burrow under skin when those clothes are worn. That's where these come from," the doctor says, pointing to several angry welts at his belt line. "Iron the clothes, Mazwika. Iron all the clothes."

The doctor's nose bleeds without warning. Red blood drips onto the sleeping child.

The doctor sits up.

"Dry air should cause a nose to bleed," he says. "No rules pertain here."

Mazwika irons.

The child wakes and watches Mazwika.

The doctor looks at the child and says, "I forgot to show

you what I picked up at the hospital this morning." He goes into the bedroom and comes out with a tiny box.

"Come have a look, Mazwika," the doctor says. Mazwika sets the charcoal iron on the ironing board and he and the child peer into the box. The child smells bitter, like tea. Inside the box is a large pink thumb. The fingernail shines clear and smooth. A mourning dove cries plaintively in the eaves. The thumb jumps. Mazwika cries, "Aya!" and the child screams and jumps back against the ironing board. The iron smashes to the cement floor. Mazwika leaps to retrieve it. The doctor laughs, unable to breathe for several seconds, then heads back to the hospital with a huge gob of tissue up his nose.

The child and Mazwika watch each other. The useless decorated gourd lies on the table. Mazwika rights it and stuffs the dried hibiscus blossoms on the kitchen table hard into its centre. The flowers crumble. Their smell is ancient. Mazwika's father says the white man emerged from the ocean. This accounts for his fish-like skin. His crabby smell. Mazwika cooks for himself corn on the cob and boiled peanuts. The doctor gets diarrhea from this combination. Mazwika does not offer any to the child. A *mundele's* jeep flies past the house and down the hill on the way to Milundu compound. Mazwika's throat sticks pained, choked with dust all afternoon.

Near dusk the doctor returns. He shuffle-steps out his screen door with the child. Light spills onto the child's shining braid. Four days she's been here.

"Shall we play hide-and-seek, Uncle Bernie?" the child cries, the thumb forgotten. The doctor plops on his front step, in this sun, no hat, and the child sits on his lap and draws her knees around him. In this heat, they'll stick together.

"Oh, Kimberly," the doctor says and hugs her. "I'll get caught."

Bernard invites Dr. Paulsen in for a late supper. He spends the early evening at the hospital, resetting the broken jaw of a small girl who was hit by a *mundele* on a motorcycle. The young Peace Corps man who hit her rides in from Molembe once a week to visit. The mother has only *saka-saka* and *fufu* at her small fire in the hospital courtyard, no liquids. Bernard and the Peace Corps man take turns bringing packaged soups imported from the States. Bernard feeds the child as she lies breathing through her nose, eyes closed. The broth chokes down her throat. The mother crouches death-still on the cement floor beside her daughter's mat.

At supper Bernard and Dr. Paulsen discuss the girl's nutrition while Kimberly rips faces in her bread. After a salad of grapefruit, passion fruit, mango, and coeur de boeuf, Bernard brings out the projector and the two men look at slides from different angles of a woman with an abdominal cyst the size of a papaya.

▰◈▰◈▰

Mazwika bends, cuts grass with his coupe-coupe in late morning heat. Dr. Schappert's wife walks slowly up the river path. The child is playing by the rabbit hutches.

"Uncle Bernie isn't home," the child calls to Mama Schappert. "Someone drove into a herd of goats and cracked his head." Loosened hair floats about her face. "One potato, two potato, three potato, four," she mutters, thumping each rabbit on the head.

Mama Schappert stands looking at the child. "Is Uncle Bernie fun to play with?" she says. Mazwika swats grass. Thwk. Thwk. Thwk. Thwk. Nurse Simbi glides by on the path above. The village rooster appears, struts over thistles, comb askew. Mazwika glimpses the doctor's white uniform heading down from the hospital at the first turn in the path. The child crouch-es, picks *ntundulu* and pops the small red berries in her mouth.

"My mom and dad say Uncle Bernie should watch me till they come back from Moliambu," the child says to the rabbit she picks from the hutch. She swings him, dangling air, by the scruff of his neck. Mazwika lays aside his coupe-coupe, carries the pineapple to the back step, and peels.

"Kimie, chick-pea!" the doctor calls from the path above. He smiles his strange smile and does a little jig, raising a swirl of dust around his white pants, then skids down the path. "Oh, hi," he says to Mama Schappert. He flips the child upside down and dangles her over his head, the rabbit now cradled in her arms. The child shouts and flails her legs.

"Oh, Kimie," Dr. Bernard drops her and shakes his head, laughing, his hand over his heart.

Mama Schappert leans against a *nkamba* tree and watches. Mazwika waters the poisonous pink blossoms of the oleander bush. Nurse Simbi passes on the path above, gliding the other way. The rooster disappears into a bar of shadow.

The doctor tweaks the child's nose and coughs. "These cooking fires," he says to no one. "Or maybe all this pollen I can't breathe but God in his sweet will. . . ."

For one dreadful moment Mama Schappert's eyes drag Mazwika's to her own. The compound fills with burning heat. A moment, then she turns and walks away. Mazwika is alone.

The doctor shuts the rabbit in the cage, grabs the child by the hand, and gallops down to the Kwilu, whinnying.

The hibiscus shimmers, violent yellow, breathtaking with colour.

After the lights go out and Kimberly is asleep, Bernard

watches her through the flickering light of the Aladdin lamp. She wavers from grey to brown, and for an instant vivid orange. The tree frogs unsettle themselves and stretch their magic feet against the bark. A thin layer of moonlight streaks the wall. Her back so frail. The shame is energy within him. Ache of hibiscus scent bleeds into thick night air.

CANADA HOUSE

Lydia, put on the wipers. How can you see the road?

Hang onto the gas barrel in the back, will you, Nick? It's rolling.

Open the window, Doug. Wet's better than hot.

Nine Mennonite Central Committee volunteers and a forty-five gallon barrel of gas stuffed in a Kombi, on their way to Vista on the ocean for the Christmas holidays. There they will transform themselves from odd pale-skinned *mundeles* into bronzed holidayers no one stares at. Five Canadian, four American expats, their pockets stuffed with one-zaire notes, together for the first time since they met at the August retreat. Together after four months in the bush: Kimpese, Mbanza-Ngungu, Mbujimi, Kijiji, Moliambu. Lydia's driving hell bent for leather. Late afternoon rain pounds the Kombi roof. Legs slick with sweat, pale skin slides first one way, then the other, as Lydia takes the corners like a madwoman. Nick (he's doing most of the yelling) squashed in the back seat between the gas barrel and Doug. If they have an accident, the Kombi will go up in instant flame.

Jees, Lydia. We're hydroplaning! Don't put on the brakes!

When I stepped into the Palais du Peuple I forgot I was in Zaire. The wedding party marched down the staircase, Mobutu's daughter dead serious. You know, brides can't smile on their wedding day.

Do you think maybe we should stop, Lydia? Judas, you can't even see the road.

She's not stopping, Nick. We've got to make the last Matadi ferry. This woman's hot to travel.

Nine MCCers, hurtling toward ten days of anonymity. Only Milton's not along. He had to stay in Kinshasa in the line up at the bank, trying to change MCC's money.

President Mobutu, now that his daughter's married off, announced four days ago that he's changing Zaire's currency. Switching colours. All five and ten zaire notes useless inside four days.

Bring all your money to the bank and have it changed, Mr. Mobutu said on radio and state television, thick black glasses underlining his authority. Yeah, right. The whole of Zaire is supposed to line up before three banks. Money already in the bank will not be lost, Mr. Mobutu said. HOWEVER, no person will be allowed to withdraw cash. For an indefinite period of time. Money that reaches the bank in time will be stamped with a government stamp. HOWEVER, Mr. Mobutu said, no individual may change more than three thousand zaires. No corporation more than twenty thousand. For three days now, lines stretch for miles. The airport's shut down. Thieves and the army march into Kinshasa.

So far Milton has stood in line for two days, spelled off for food and sleep. Noon of the first day, the bank president throws open a second story window, and shouts, The bank has not received new money yet. Show patience. Please.

That evening the line still hasn't moved. The army steps through the crowd and chains the bank doors. People stand in line all night. Nick changes Milton off. You can't imagine, Nick

says. The muggy air ripe with terrible smells from sweating uri-
nating bodies. Midafternoon the crowd rushes the doors.
Attempts to tear off the chain. Tramples children. Twelve people
dead. Gendarmes appear, cracking people on the head and
shoulders with their guns.

Lydia took Milton food before they left this afternoon.
The missionaries in Kinshasa will spell him off. Some people
in line have had no food or water in almost fifty hours, Lydia
says. Tonight they'll get a drink, standing in pouring rain. The
old man in front of Milton opened wide his tattered suitcase
and flung money in the air. Paper bills rained the street, flut-
tered down the sewers. Not a person in the crowd reached to
catch one.

Fuckez-vous, Zaire, Doug says. Hey, he says from the dimness of the back seat. Let's play twenty questions. But everybody
wants to talk.

What a sight. Zairian wedding guests stuffing food in their
suit pockets, inside *nleles*. A man poured beer over a woman's
hands so she could wash off the turkey grease. I am not making
fun. Lord, it was scary. They must have never in their lives seen
so much food.

Lydia, that's a sharp curve up ahead.

Anybody got an orange?

For God's sake, Lydia. Slow. Down!

Well, at least the army's out of Kimpese. In Kimpese, the
military played war in November. One morning at prayers, the
school préfet announced their coming. Mama's don't go to your
fields, he said, you may be robbed or shot. You realize how
bands of robbers can mix with the military.

The bands of robbers *are* the fucking military.

You're going to have to clean up your language, Doug, if
you go the ministry route.

The army harassed students. One househelp mama was
thrown in jail for not carrying her carte d'identité. She paid one

hundred and twenty zaires, two month's salary, and the gendarmes let her go.

The nine MCCers don't stop talking, packed together in this hurtling Kombi. They cling to English. Everybody has a story.

Hand me a mango.

What about cholera?

No one knows. I'd wash the fruit.

This road is dangerous. Potholed. Doorless vehicles break down. People abandon them and walk away. Even on a clear day, Lydia would be in danger of driving into a parked jalopy as they round a corner.

Villages skim by. Kasangulu, Madimba, Songololo. Brown banana heaps along the roadway. Lightning flashes, lighting up Zaire's wet red earth. Velvet greens, primary yellows. People appear out of nowhere on the road. Lydia swerves. And suddenly, before them, the narrow, picturesque streets of Matadi, the town lying flat against a hillside. Dusk. They queue up for the last ferry. Velma has to pee. There are no bathrooms and at last she squats beside a plant. The Zairians don't pay attention.

Somewhere in the long line behind them, the Belgian ambassador to Zaire pulls up in a limousine. He sends his driver up to talk to the ferry operator. The ambassador's white, he's government. He thinks he has the right to jump the queue. Doug starts a catcall. Hey, fartface, wait your turn. The Zairians are delighted. Joyful insults fly in Kikongo, Linguala, French. The ambassador sits, red-faced and furious, harboured in his grand car. The ferry operator, buoyed up by this united show of force, actually shakes his head.

Lydia manoevers the Kombi onto the creaking ferry. Women, returning from market with their unsold plantains and peanuts, crowd around the Kombi. Doug buys nine small greasy doughnuts. A one-legged man hops up the ferry plank. A woman dances, stroking music from the ribs of a Fanta bottle.

A child joins her, her hand caressing beats from a small drum. Children peer in the Kombi windows, but the nine MCCers look out at the green hills behind them to the dots of smouldering cooking fires and the livid ambassador who doesn't make the ferry. He'll have to spend the night in queue.

A half hour later they drive off the other side. They're on the last stretch.

What're we having for Christmas dinner, Lydia?

Rooster. The best we can do.

Mmmmm. Fresh cock, Doug says. The MCCers pelt him with oranges.

Eventually the Kombi falls silent. Nick calls through the darkness, Lydia, you awake?

Oh, sure, Lydia says. You think I'd fall asleep? If I hit someone we'll all be beaten to death.

Well, if you hit someone, Lydia, Doug says, just keep driving.

The rain abates. Someone opens a window. Their legs dry off, but nine pairs of blue jean shorts are still heavy with sweat.

They pull into Canada House at Vista, ten o'clock and moonlit, scramble from the Kombi and race to the beach. Nine *mundeles* gaze out across that dark blue water and try to picture America. Their throats ache they try so hard to make it happen. Hot African wind. The beach stretches forever. Fine white sand. Ochre cliffs. Crashing Atlantic waves. Nine *mundeles* can't imagine: the Atlantic Ocean at the mouth of the Zaire River. The wind cools. A pirogue slowly passes, hauling a fish net. As they breathe in the sea wind and the salt sea smell, a gull's cry, something happens:

There are old slave market grounds a few kilometres from here. Abandoned chains and ankle bracelets and an enormous rendering pot. The nine MCCers laugh and chatter. They will find the grounds tomorrow. They will chain each other up, take pictures which they will send to the other side of this dark endless ocean. Who knows, each thinks, what might happen in a foreign country? And this thought sprays away hostile students, a language they barely understand, the endless stares, the bitter loneliness. Just this moment they remember only that tomorrow is Christmas.

Nine MCC bodies, stiff with four months of unwelcomed expectations, unfold, loosen, and relax.

Nine MCC *mundeles* forget they have to spray for cockroaches, forget they have to put gas pellets in the flour to kill the worms. All that's ten days from now. Just this moment, the shouts, the insults, the sting of small stones merge and float away through the hot night.

The nine MCCers kick their toes in sand, return, joyous, enervated, yes, horny, to Canada House. They retreat to their respective sleeping quarters where bats move in the walls. They make love, slipping in and through each others' bodies.

All night the bats hear their anxious flutter.

A CHAMELEON
IN THE GARDEN

Imagine a fair April morning in a western Canadian city. Sky scraped blue. Cool sun. A train whistle decorating the morning air. A robin calling. A Zairian woman seats herself on a patio in a suburban back yard. Warm air tinged lightly with exhaust fumes. Before her, a piled plate of waffles smothered in strawberries and whipped cream. Deep-fried mushrooms line a platter. In her pocket is a letter to her mother which she will not mail. A white boy swings on his patio chair beside the woman, reciting National Hockey League statistics. The sun flits behind a cloud, emerges. Sharpens the outline of the woman, eating. The boy's small sister eats beside him, fine brown hair braided in seven braids, all caught up in a red scarf at her neck. She kneels on a chair to reach the table. The three eat together. A large green rooster stares out from a Kellogg's Corn Flakes box.

Or imagine the same city in November. Five months earlier. Snowflakes shiver to the ground. Minus twelve degrees. Pale winter dusk. The same young woman, still thin, imagines herself in snow. Sees a black woman sloshing through manioc flour whiteness. She walks alone, returning from English lessons at the Mennonite Centre for Newcomers. No one in the streets. Until her arrival in this western city she has never been alone. Never once in her twenty-four years. She watches herself now because she cannot help it, but also to create company. She sees her underarms squeezed tight against the cold. Coat hanging ajar. No. Ajar is for doors. But she is learning. A young Zairian woman in a long red coat from the thrift store, a long red scarf. She sees the woman tilt her black face, scan the sky. This city, perhaps this country, has no stars. No ancestors live here. The city lights mirage in dry pink-yellow swirls. Like the lights of the *mundele* doctor's imported Christmas tree in the young woman's village. In the young woman's head, that small smoking village is dissolving. She watches herself, alone on a city street, struggling to hold this image, to grab at stars. Black. Vanga village in her head. Black, except for the occasional flicker of a cooking fire, or the pale gleam of a *mundele's* flashlight. The young woman knows that night here in Calgary Alberta Canada means day in Vanga village, but since late September her village has slid into permanent night. She receives no letters, sends none. Who can afford stamps? And anyway, she is no longer sure that Zairian world exists. Instead, the woman eats. She eats. She eats doughnuts by the dozen. She eats stale dry peanuts by the glassful.

Imagine the noise of this city in Simbi's ears. She wakes to explosions of mystery toilet flush garburator grind howl of Vacuflo dishwasher swoosh coffee gurgle windy popcorn popper Super Nintendo beep. In Vanga village a person can hear a drum's hollow twang, the *nzenzi* hum, a fruit bat's cry, the Kwilu river shuck against its shores.

Canada is a colourless land, no violent beauty. Dull pines replace flame trees, brown back yards vanish Zaire's brilliant grasses. No streams. Sometimes a solitary tree. Here the host father irons his wife's clothes as if he were a servant in his own house. At Vanga village, missionaries float on their backs down the Kwilu River from Linungu Beach. Small children watch the splash of hippos in McKwanga Bay.

Children in Canada hoe no garden, fetch no water, care for no babies, prepare no food. Simbi rides light rail transit to English school at night. Alone. Nothing is as it might be. Nothing *is*.

Imagine the September Simbi arrives in Canada. An autumn rainstorm. Her host family has deposited her host father's mother, soon to be an ancestor, in a two-roomed flat in a large building on the far side of town. And left her. The family visits. Every person here is old. The children race empty wheelchairs down dark corridors, bang on doors and run. When they demand stories, the aged read. A million grey droplets slant to earth. In Vanga village, rain has no individuality. Rain slides. Lightning strikes the préfet of the school across his back. The man is killed. Lightning strikes a village boy across the foot. He loses flesh. Such things never happen here, the host family tells Simbi. It rains. It rains. Streets in Calgary Alberta Canada are awash. Within four days three people are struck by lightning: a man on a golf course, a woman at a bus stop, a small boy riding his bicycle in a back alley. There is much *ndoki* in this country, Simbi says. There is no witchcraft in Canada, Simbi's host mother says. Such things do not happen here.

Simbi says, Ahh.

This city has storm sewers. They refuse to work. Streets cascade water. Someone drowns in an underpass. The basement of her hosts' unsuspecting suburban house floods. Simbi helps sop up the water. She is so happy. Calgary Alberta Canada is like home.

The rain stops. Simbi's host family drives her to Lake Louise to prove that Canada has nature. They take with them the host father's mother. So old, with clicking teeth and wobbly skin. Before they reach Lake Louise, the gearshift linkage breaks. They spend the afternoon in a garage in Banff. What's happening? Simbi's host mother says. Why all this bad luck? Bad spirits, Simbi says. Someone has captured ancestral spirits and put them to use. Don't be ridiculous, Simbi's host mother says. The wild-haired old lady in the back seat, swathed in blankets, grins at Simbi.

Imagine Simbi's dreams. In what language does she dream? She cannot tell.

The tall thin dried-up woman, her host father's mother, dies. Simbi gathers her friends from Vanga village. They wail, they swoon, they shuffle the dance of death, they give the old lady a respectful send-off into ancestral life. Her host father, the wife, the children, circle the television and chew Cheesies.

Or, Simbi's host father drives her to the airport in his fancy car. It's raining Zaire rain. So, Simbi, you're going to America with your host man? people say. Yes, Simbi says. How will she get the money? Worries, worries, leaves the passenger door *ajar*. The rain-soaked seat stains with salted buttered popcorn. Where did it come from? Her host man so angry, turns from the airport, makes Simbi drive the car in unfamiliar streets, criticizes her left turns, says he's decided not to take her to America after all.

Or, Simbi enters the dimness of her hosts' house. She must clean, hunts cleaning solvent, rags, discovers the house is sold. It turns into an ugly dark apartment shack, stale-smelling stairwells curve. Simbi is so ashamed to live in this place crawling with cockroaches, army ants and snakes, the smell of sweat. Simbi's host mother meets Simbi on the apartment stairs, takes her hands. The walls turn a lovely shade of green. They're made of forest vines. I live here! Simbi says, so joyous. The host woman smiles and says, Perhaps you do.

Simbi sits at breakfast mornings with her host family, watches them spoon cornflakes into their mouths. Ancestors keep track of the living through dreams. Dreams bless or curse. If a person dreams about another person, that first person wishes the other evil. Don't let Vanessa play near water, Simbi says. I had a dream.

The host father's mother dies. The family tells Simbi there is no need for her to attend the funeral. Simbi goes anyway. The church building closes in, its windows hidden by painted glass. Simbi sees her shape reflected in these windows. A translucent shadow. Ornate benches. Benches with backs. No stains on the roof. The large church room is silent. Heavy, heavy air. No one sways or wails. No one burns *musangu-sangu* and hops over it. No one sits for hours with the body, waving away flies. Simbi cannot breathe. She is a hippo, running against water.

<hr />

On this April morning eight months later Simbi sits on her hosts' patio. Watching. She sees herself so clearly. She eats strawberries, mushrooms, no thought of goat sauce dripping from her fingers. She refuses beans for lunch. Beans are food of the poor. Simbi has stopped asking her host mother how she got a husband; she watches television commercials. She has learned the walk that causes men to drop the morning paper and chase a girl with flowers, she chews the gum that makes men throw back their heads and laugh. Simbi speaks to men now, walks beside men, wears blue jeans. She rarely braids her hair. Fears only, perhaps, her lack of fear.

Simbi does however braid the child's hair. The mother likes this. The child does not care. Tiny plaited braids coil like snake cables. The child sits if Simbi recites Zairian names. Bulungu. Molembe. Kimwanza. Lubumbelele, Ngangungu, Ngomboco, Diawambanzila, Lubumbashe. The child laughs. The child's father's name is Hoyt. The child finds this normal. Sometimes when the child fidgets and begins to struggle before Simbi's braids are done, Simbi paints for the child frozen moments. A fruit bat swings, crying, through a stalactite cave near Kimpese village. A market stall explodes with colour: purple eggplant, rusty palm nuts, green caterpillars, pyramids of orangey-red tomatoes. A man in a hand-carved canoe rocks in the Kwilu's gentle current, waiting to ferry another man across to the far shore. A small boy on an empty football field balances a chameleon on an outstretched stick.

The child demands to know how a chameleon looks. The mother gets a book out of the library. She sits by the child while Simbi braids.

Chameleons, this book is called. *Dragons in the Trees.* The child turns her head to listen. Everywhere in Africa chameleons watch. Their eyes swivel, looking for food or danger. Their skin adjusts pattern and colour to their surroundings. Chameleons can change colour in just a few seconds. Chameleons are able to look in two directions at once. A chameleon's tongue is its most amazing feature.

"I want a chameleon," the child cries, "a chameleon in my garden." Begs to go to the pet store. But the host family finds no chameleon in the city of Calgary Alberta Canada.

"Chameleons die when faced with life in a terrarium," the pet store clerk says. Without warning, Simbi experiences a horror so complete she fears that she will kill the child, or surely kill herself. The moment passes.

What do you do to kill time in Africa? the host boy asks Simbi. Simbi feels her body grow large with this new language. How can she answer? Her home is timeless, there is no time to kill. In Zaire no one runs, glancing at watches, crying instructions over shoulders, typing furiously at small computers, heating food in two minutes or less, leaving children with other people's children while they rush to kill time. Simbi is learning to move within this time. She has learned to stir up contents from the bottom, learned the deft wrist action with which one scrapes a bowl.

In four more months, Simbi will have her picture taken

with these North Americans. She will gather her clothes, her five watches, her hair ornaments and fly to Toronto, to Belgium, board Sabena Airways, dip down in Lagos, and speed through clouds to Kinshasa. A small Mission Aviation Fellowship plane will drop her at last at the runway a kilometre from Vanga village where she will pile all her belongings on her head and walk through the ancestors' breaths, slipping off her shoes after the first few metres to feel again Zaire's hot sand between her toes, will jump across a thick red column of army ants, gaze up at the green pods hanging from a giant baobab, and, as she nears the village outskirts, will catch the sharp scent of limes, rotting on the ground, will smell the stench of manioc spread out to dry.

Imagine, years after, under Zaire's fierce sun, there will remain within Simbi a fine thread of memory, a fragile umbilical cord stretching across an endless ocean. To put herself to sleep some night perhaps Simbi, an older woman now, will imagine a young black woman, a Zairian woman at a breakfast table in a North American country, imagining a water hyacinth float down the Kwilu. Beside her, a red-combed rooster staring at the future from a box of cornflakes. Perhaps Simbi will imagine a young Zairian woman in a North American bed, straining for the sharp whistle of a nightjar, for the chew of termites, for the whispered footstep of a thief. And she will lie on her sleeping mat in Vanga village, a middle-aged woman, looking both directions, faint with desire for a language in which to dream.

JIGGER

Young girls and young wimmin
They set my heart singin'
They make life worth livin, they do

Tony Lauber is digging jiggers from his feet, drinking *malafu*, and composing a new song, when he hears the refectory women at the round cement cistern just behind his house, stealing water. Four o'clock. Right on the nose. Tony drops his needle (he's dug down to the white sack which is still attached to his left foot), takes a slurp of *malafu* from his jam jar, and clubfoots toward the bedroom so he won't disturb the jiggers. That's all he needs. Parasites bursting their sacks and boring into his feet. One sack in the ball of each foot. His right foot pings his guitar case lying on the floor at the hall entrance. The women don't hear.

Tony, you're a lucky man, Tony Lauber says to himself when he reaches the bedroom door. He presses against the wall, under the hole in the ceiling (coolest place in the house). He can see straight through the bedroom window to the women on the ladder, a natural landscape. And they can't see him. They think no one knows they steal the water the préfet has trucked up to Tony's cistern. They could spend forty minutes twice a day trekking to the Source, then back up the hill with pails of slopping water on their heads. No, they're smart, these women; they've learned. Time is money — they steal his water instead.

> Young wimmin' and young girls
> As precious as rare pearls

The two women on the ladder wear *nleles*. One brown, crisscrossed with a dotting of yellow flowers, the other purple with a pinkish-blue paisley pattern. The higher woman lifts an old galvanized pail overflowing with water from the top of the cistern. Some slops out as she raises it high over the cistern lip, and lands with a splat on the woman's head and chest below. The other woman on the ladder gives a gaspy shriek before reaching up for the pail and handing it down to a third woman on the ground. She wears a red checkered Western sundress with a pin in the shoulder strap.

"Time ees moneey," they call softly to each other (which is what Tony tells the students in his English class). In America, time is money. It's what he tells the vendeur who sells him his homemade palm wine. All three women bend over, snorting and gasping, hands stuffed in their mouths, and Tony Lauber can see three bits of cleavage.

> They make all my wild'st dreams come true

The outsides of Tony's feet are beginning to ache, standing clubfooted as he is, so before the third pail is filled, he waddles back to the living room couch, picks up his needle, and digs for three minutes. One sack out. He lays the small intact black-dotted thing on the floor and leans his right foot over his left knee. Digs. This is more awkward.

> Adorned in spring dresses
> Like mystical goddesses

Beat's off. Four thirty-five. Tony doesn't think he can handle Antoine's baked beans and *fufu* again.

Tony, my man, he says. What say we pop out the second sack later and do a loop to Vanga, see what's cookin'. He has a variety of homes he can choose from. He could go to Dr. Schappert's to get his feet checked, Stanley Jepson's to borrow a hoe, Monica Katz' to discuss teaching methods, Dudley Vigoren's to book a flight out of here June thirtieth. (He may bum around Europe for the summer to cool off.) Bernard Elliot, the new Canadian doctor, he writes off the list. Weird bugger. Bakes seven different kinds of bread on his days off. Oatmeal porridge bread. Whole wheat molasses bread. Herb bread. Day in and day out, that's his supper. Bread and homemade marmalade and guavas. Not Tony's idea of a meal. Anyway he has those missionary kids swarming his place all the time — playing leapfrog and word games, telling dumb jokes. If Tony makes it by five-thirty, states his business, chats a bit, it will be dark and six o'clock and supper will be on. Must be over a week now since he's stopped by the Schapperts.

Edith Schappert doesn't look real chummy, in fact her mouth pulls tight as a shoestring when Tony roars into Vanga, and up the path to the Schappert house that overlooks the Kwilu. He cuts the motor and swings his leg over the bike.

"Your hubby home?" he calls.

"Dr. Schappert is still up at the hospital," Edith says severely. "Someone just fell out of a palm tree."

"Why, I'll just wait beneath this one then," Tony says, and

sinks into the dust under the nearest palm, then jumps up in mock terror, hand tilted over his eyebrows, and gazes through the fronds.

"Hate to be crushed by a falling *malafu* man," Tony says because Edith didn't get the joke. Still doesn't. Edith disapproves of Tony drinking *malafu*. She disapproves of Tony. Expatriates are here in Zaire to set an example. She turns her back on Tony and starts gathering wash from the line behind the rabbit cages.

"Dr. Schappert is bound to be very late," she says. "The man's broken all his limbs." "In our yard," she adds to herself. She's dropped a blue blouse and a pair of panties. Tony waits till she's almost at the door, then gathers them up and trails her, arriving at the moment she is fighting with the screen door latch over her load of wash.

"At your service," Tony says, bowing, and swings open the door. Edith staggers through and Tony steps in behind her, the door latches, and he's made it. The house is dim and cool. He follows her into the living room where she drops her load of wash, then politely hands her the large pair of washed-out panties with sagging elastic.

"Way Antoine pounds the hell out of my underwear is a killer too," Tony says. The woman doesn't look good. Sweating, a sticky loop of grey hair falling into her eyes. Severe. She looks severe. Doesn't thank him for his gallantries. The Schappert's cat hops on the wash pile and lazily stretches her claws.

Tony can smell *biteke-teke*. He was hoping for something Western.

"Use up your South African chicken then?" he asks Edith, leaning in the kitchen doorway, watching her scratch at something in a kettle on the gas burner. Tony knows Edith doesn't like to be reminded the missionaries eat food shipped from South Africa. She doesn't answer. If Dr. Schappert will be so late, why is she cooking supper now?

"Need a hand with anything?"

"No." And her shoulders bunch so tight Tony has to rub his neck. Maybe he should have tried the Vigoren's. Edith turns off the gas bomb and goes out the door, and Tony's left standing in the kitchen with the cat crawling his pant leg. Tony guesses she is pissed off with her husband for coming home so late. Maybe he should see how Dudley Vigoren's house smells. A pilot can fly in any food supplies.

Tony's turning to go (she may be bugged, but leaving him here alone in her house is downright rude) when the front gate opens and Schappert's daughter, sixteen? what the hell's her name? Melissa? Miranda? Melissa? comes up the walk. Tony wonders what she's doing here in Vanga. She goes to boarding school in Kinshasa, lives in the Baptist Hostel there, that's where Tony first necked with her — the night he arrived in Africa, the night he got his passport stolen. Melissa's looking up at her mother's face in the deepening dusk (her mother is a tall woman), then at the house. She gives a little laugh and skip-walks up the path. If Tony can believe her story, a hippo bit her foot when she was small. Tony decides *biteke-teke* will do just fine.

As Melissa slams the screen door, the generator cuts in and the kitchen is filled with dazzling brightness. The cat bounds across the kitchen floor and leaps into Melissa's arms. Tony blinks and blinks again and Melissa shows her straight white teeth and her face dances spots and she says, "Did you miss me, you little tabby you. You staying for supper, Tony?" She walks close by him, nearly brushes him as she heads for the cupboard.

"Well, if that's an invitation. . . ." The screen door slams. Hard. Edith is back.

"Will Dad be late, Mom? I'll set the table for three."

"Here, let me," Tony says and sets the silverware around the plates, all the while smiling at Edith.

There is chicken, cold chicken — that's why he didn't smell it. Melissa (she's probably seventeen) eats a drumstick from between her fingers and then licks the grease off. By now he's found out why she's here. There was some two-day holiday tacked onto the weekend at the American School in Kinshasa. A holiday Tony's school here at Milundu doesn't honour. His luck. And she leaves tomorrow. He doesn't have much time then. Melissa gives the cat a piece of dark meat and she nibbles daintily. Melissa tells some story about jumping off the tree swing in the Baptist Hostel yard, describes the view over the broken-bottle-lined compound wall while you're sitting in the baobab, trying to get your nerve up, describes how your heart gets left behind as the swing drops six feet before the rope jerks taut.

"The family's going to blame someone for that man's fall," Edith says, scraping her food about her plate.

"You'll have to try it, Tony," Melissa giggles, "next time you're in Kinshasa." She's remembering the last time.

"What misfortune that he fell in our yard."

"The swing's just for kids, really," Melissa says to her mother.

Her mother chews her chicken and *biteke-teke* and never once makes eye contact with Tony, not even when she says, "I'm sure Tony would like it then."

Tony helps himself to a large slice of breast.

"Want a motorcycle spin?" Tony asks as they clear the dishes, he and Melissa. Edith has disappeared into the living room where they now hear a whoomp whoomp whoooomp that Tony cannot identify. Neither, it appears, can Melissa. Her smile bounces out at him, and she says, "What *is* my mother doing?"

They squeeze through the doorway together with the cat (Melissa's developed some in the last three months) in time to see Edith murder a small bat with a violent blow from Melissa's tennis racket. Then she sinks onto the couch and sucks deep gulps of air. The cat whaps the lifeless bat between her paws.

"Mom! Where did it come from?" Melissa asks, from the safety of Tony's side.

"It infiltrated the fireplace, Melissa. Do you think I invited it in?"

Really, Tony figures, he should be on his way.

⬛◣◢⬜◣◢⬛

The minute the motor roars to life and Tony feels that gangly body pressed against his, Coconut, the cat, munched between them (Melissa insists the animal enjoys motorcycle rides) the next verse comes to him all at once. He sings even though he cannot hear himself.

> We meet and start talkin'
> I suggest we go walkin'
> And you know what that can lead to
> Yes, I'm quite persistent
> But the girls aren't resistant (great line!)
> They line up for me in a queue.

"Are you *singing?*" Melissa yells in his ear, and her brown hair tangles around his ear. He can feel her breasts beneath his shoulder blades.

"Got any better ideas?" he shouts back.

"Yes," Melissa giggles, but says nothing more. The warm night air shivers past them. Their headlights illuminate ant hills, palm nut shelves, the *kapoc* tree, its silky fluff shining silver in the darkness, and then the bike makes a sudden dip that leaves Tony's stomach behind. They coast the hill (while the confounded cat gallops his back) and bump across the wooden bridge and up the incline to Milundu.

Little cooking fires dot the compound, lick out at them. "I don't think Mom would like this," Melissa says. "This is so romantic."

Tony cuts the motor and the bike grinds to a stop before his house. He leads Melissa inside and she stands in the dark by the living room couch until he lights his Aladdin lamp. Cockroaches scurry. Melissa's foot clinks Tony's *malafu* jar. The wick burns high and Melissa says, "Ooooh."

"It's okay," Tony says. "It's no big deal," and he pushes her down on the couch and kisses her. Melissa says, "Ooooh," again, only a little breathier. She tastes like chicken grease. Tony licks his lips.

"You taste like chicken grease," Melissa says.

Tony takes a gulp of palm wine.

Melissa knows a lot for sixteen. She knows a lot for seventeen. Maybe she's coming eighteen. Coconut joins them, rubs her body against Tony's legs, jumps on Tony's back, nuzzles his armpit. Lord, is the cat in heat? The mantle is burning up again. Tony reaches out to turn the wick down. Melissa hangs on giggling, hooks her legs around Tony's, and he has to grab the table for support. Midlurch, he steps on Coconut, who jumps back with a peevish yowl and heads for the kitchen.

Tony balances himself and kisses Melissa. Passionately. He likes to think adverbs and adjectives during his forays. Feverishly. Helps his song writing. He'll probably sell a few songs when he gets back to Kansas. He's unhooking her bra when Melissa sits up so suddenly he bumps his nose on her cheekbone. She twists her arm around him and stares at her watch over his shoulder. "Dad'll be home any minute. Will Mom be stewing!"

> But these girls have mothers
> And fathers and brothers

THE COCK'S EGG

(Melissa doesn't, but it rhymes)
Who can't see what stage they've passed to

All passion leaves Tony in one disappointing swoop, because her mention of Dr. Schappert makes him think of the balls of his feet which he is grinding into the hard cement floor; the right sack will be broken. Tony groans.

"It's okay," Melissa says, and licks him, cat-like, under his chin. "You're really turned on, aren't you," and she giggles. Well, maybe fourteen, fifteen.

Tony likes the word desire, and appetite, he decides as they bump over the washed-out road to Vanga. This time Melissa is doing the singing. Tony can't make out the words, but the tune sounds like the Zairian national anthem. Da da da da da da da da da da da. . . .

But me, I keep lookin'
No desire to get hooked in

It isn't working. He can't compose with Melissa moaning in his ear.

When they pull up to Schappert's house, Tony thinks better of going in with Melissa to talk to Dr. Schappert about his jiggers. He can see the man, head bowed over his dinner plate, through the glaring light from the kitchen window. Edith standing over him, one looking as cheerful as the other.

"Good night, Tony."

Tony revs the engine.

"Rrrrrrrr," Melissa says.

By the time Tony gets back to Milundu it is eleven o'clock.

He has a dull headache. Probably getting malaria. He decides right then and there not to go into class tomorrow, so he makes his way to the SS Five classroom and feels for chalk. He writes, "Je suis malade. Classe annulé," on the bumpy chalkboard. His stomach is queasy. Edith's chicken. Next time he'll try the Vigoren's. A fruit bat swoops his path as he walks through the insect-humming air to his house, and he thinks of Edith Schappert, crouched triumphant over her dead bat; Antoine is reported to have served poisoned *chikwanga* to the last English teacher for failing his daughter. Maybe Edith borrowed his recipe. Tony pulls off his clothes without brushing his teeth and falls into bed.

ER ER ER ER ERRRRRR tears into Tony's sleep and shakes him into dim morning light that tells him the time must be four-thirty. Goddamn rooster. Clucking now beside the water cistern right outside his window. He should slit its throat. Who says roosters don't roar. His head aches dismally. He reaches for his alarm clock and the motion brings a wave of nausea to his throat and now there's a scratching and yowling at his bedroom door. Melissa's damned cat! They forgot to take her back. The rooster roars again, then flutters off screeching when Tony heaves a sandal at the window.

"Get out o' here," he yells at the door, but Coconut is determined to pay him back for his neglect, or for stepping on her hindquarters last night. Scrape, scrape, scrape. Beastly animal. Tony flips back the covers. If he's to get any sleep this morning he might as well let her in. He throws himself from the bed and a spotty blackness crashes up to meet him. He feels along the wall and opens the bedroom door.

Coconut, desperate with anticipation, flings herself into the room, and claws up the curtains, meowing loudly. Has the world gone mad? He has to lie down. Tony has just sunk back into the rumpled heap of covers, bowels churning, head bursting, when the cat drops on the bed. Fighting vertigo, Tony sits up, grabs her by the stomach and lets her fly. With a last screech, Coconut squats and drops a load of foul smelling shit, and Tony is stumbling for the bathroom which doesn't work because it's the dry season, and retching into the empty toilet bowl.

When Tony heads for the bedroom fifteen minutes later, he sees he cannot get back into bed. He's left the bedroom window open and the refectory women are stealing water. They're giggling and holding their noses, and Tony realizes the smell from the cat shit pile is wafting out the window. He lies down on the cement floor in the hallway, and the smooth cold floor is good on the back of his head.

Melissa's cat, relieved of her burden, comes purring down the hall. Her wide green eyes glitter. She pauses, one paw uplifted, raises her head, and Tony knows she smells rats in the roof. Zairians eat cats, Tony tells her. She just steps daintily around him. I should put you out the door, see how long you'd last, he tells her, but that is difficult from where he lies on the floor, so instead he dreams of water, his water swishing clandestinely in the women's buckets, a drink of cool, boiled water to rinse the taste of retching from his throat, pure water to cleanse the cat shit from the floor. He pictures Edith Schappert, waist deep in the cement tank behind the church, dunking converts, purging souls. He is struck suddenly by the transforming power of water.

Tony Lauber, you're a fool, Tony says to himself. Get yourself off this floor and ask those women to bring you water. Tony rises to his knees and crawls in a wide arc past the cat droppings to the window.

At Vanga hospital compound seven kilometres away, Dr. Schappert is diagnosing the *malafu* man with the broken limbs. The man is paralyzed from the neck down. "Perhaps he was behind in his deliveries," the chief of Vanga tells the doctor. "A buyer of his wine may have cast a spell. The culprit will be searched out and punished."

Dr. Schappert lifts a prayer to God to grant him patience, and begins to tell the chief the accident occurred because the man's safety belt was carelessly tied. Edith Schappert, newly arrived at the hospital with lunch for her husband, offers the chief a guava. *"Malafu* brings nothing but grief," she says.

"The accident happened in your yard?" the chief asks politely.

"We do not allow *malafu* to be gathered from our palm trees," Edith says sternly. "The man was trespassing. Coconut, our cat," she adds, "was chasing a stray rooster. The rooster flew into the palm tree and frightened the man." Dr. Schappert glances at his watch. The chief of Vanga listens with interest. "Coconut caught the rooster by the foot as the bird flew down, but he spun away."

"Ah, it is so clear," the chief of Vanga says. "The weaver of this spell took the form of a rooster. Thanks to your cat, the sorcerer will have a sore foot. Perhaps infection, perhaps he is already showing signs of sickness." Edith Schappert helps herself to the doctor's last guava. "A tribunal will be held," the chief says. "Here we are Christian. Such *ndoki* shall not go unpunished."

"Citoyen, if I may—" Dr. Schappert begins, but Edith Schappert interrupts her husband.

·   "Tony Lauber — the young teacher at Milundu," she adds for the chief's sake, "is known to drink palm wine." She shakes her head in pity. Then says suddenly to her husband, "Did I ask you, Daniel, next time Tony drops in for supper if you might take a peek at his foot. Last night he was limping." She smiles at the chief, offers him water from her jug.

"Masa," Tony calls. "Apportez-moi du *masa,"* but his voice is weak and scratchy, and the devious women are already winding along the footpath to the refectory where they will prepare the students' breakfast, and the students are rising and struggling into their blue Western pants and white long-sleeved shirts, ready for a another day of learning.

Tony Lauber is seized with a bout of vomiting. Outside, inexplicably, there is a slow burn of rain.

I SEEK. EMIGRATION

Africa. A free ka "- nada is the prairie cowboy Canada is the
Yukon miner." Dr. Coffin Elementary School on a warm May
Calgary evening ten years after Africa twenty after Saskatchewan
a stifling gym parents peer through dimness to the stage their
children, one small girl recently arrived from Texas, "Canada
hey Canada Let's see it Uh huh uh huh Let's see it Uh huh!" A
dark gym stuffed with parents throat-choked parents who have
not felt a patriotic stirring in how many years, "Our — flag —
is — blowing in the sky It sets our hearts aflame with pride We
live in Canada We're talking Canada!"

I watch our children: Jordan and Madeleine, watch Feraz,
Kalpesh, Rodriquez, Tamise, "It's blowing free For you and
me. . . ."

At night I dream.

I climb wide wooden stairs leading to a roof silent Zairians
line these stairs watch me swim deep into stillness pass a man

THE COCK'S EGG

tied to the step a metal collar hands bound by heavy ropes woman's arm twists lace of swaying bodies shadow violent yellow reds she lunges wide knife clasped in her toes a human semicircle chains round my tongue flapping soundless.

In the morning, my sweat-soaked bed holds slow motion movement. A braid of blackness. Like poured oil.

"Peuple grand, peuple libre à jamais." A free ka. Milundu, Zaire. Africa. Four hundred students stand to attention in dawn's first light. Waving before them, the Zairian flag. Wilting in forty degree humidity. Another verse? "Tricolore enflamme nous du feu sacré." Their flag. Sacred fire. Red flaming torch encircled in yellow flanked by avocado green. And Doug Markum, newly arrived refugee worker, arrested, jailed, expelled from the country for joking the flag held four colours. Reference to that fierce black fist grasping the flaming torch. "Oyez! Oyez, Mobutu! Eiiii. Oyez, Zaire!"

Mees, you help my brother about letter in university for Canada? "We have a voice that is calling telling all the world we're willing To welcome them to this great land And — that's — what — Ca-na-da — is." Mees, how many toilets one person own in Canada? You eat meat all day in Canada? Mees, how many cars you drive in Canada? You abandon your mothers in large buildings when they grow old? Mees how much your husband pay to own you? Mees, I buy your blue jeans — when you go?

At night I dream.

I enter an elevator slide up silent Canadians scrunched backs faces averted pass cold space an ice wind elevator door grinds ajar people step through winter clamps thick coats against a black-white blur viewed through blue bitter smoking bald man puffy petulant face hooks breaths I can't breathe painted metal chains tense bodies staring forward my tongue flapping soundless.

In the morning, my cold bed a white-out backwash. A clutch of dryness cracking under frost and sun.

"I have welcomed the dawn from the fields of Saskatchewan." Sass. Catch. Eiii. Saskatchewan. That sassy two-storey Guernsey schoolhouse a solitary temptress of learning on a windswept prairie. White-ice November afternoon. Miss Schellenberg shushes us. We hold stillness in our desks. She touches the radio dial. CBC school broadcast. Leopoldville, the Congo. Bicycle bells jangle. Tires crunch. I absent myself into noisy street throngs heat the joyous cacophony goat wails smoke-scented cries market bartering heel-calloused feet honey-citrus-textured music of Africa bone-light lizard-scuttle splash of hot pick-pocket wind gourd clutter bright tomato pyramids pebble-scatter of desire coming apart. In me. The radio crackles. Miss Schellenberg leans across her battered desk to close us into silence. The dull afternoon chills my stockinged legs. It's Friday. Two-thirty. Grade six Red Cross meeting. I take my place, the secretary's chair, at the teacher's worn desk next to the Red Cross president. Next to the radio, still warm. My fingers curl against the metal, secretly cocoon its hum. I look out across the school yard, across that frozen space down to the swings, the sidewalk that ends at Spence's grocery, the hub of my Saskatchewan existence. The Congo, transformed.

At this moment, I lift my hand from my smudged page and

step through the second story window. I leave behind my father's chicken farm with its strutting cocks. I leave behind Guernsey. I disappear behind Spence's grocery. My narrow world refracts: before me, a sheet of perfect falling water; beyond, a clash of brilliant greens, and the dissolving image of a blood-red cock. The scent of bird. Wind-whiff of bougainvillea. My body shakes, a faint but steady shimmer. The *nlele* swirls and twists about my legs. I kick free, spread my wings, shiver a moment on the edge of Vampa Falls, the Congo, Zaire, Africa, the world. A gust of lemon-swallowed wind. I fling my pen. And glide.

Rosemary Nixon

Rosemary Nixon's stories have appeared in literary magazines across Canada. A winner in *Grain* short fiction competition and *Prairie Fire* short fiction competition, Nixon has also published recently, in *Matrix, The New Quarterly, NeWest Review. absinthe,* and in the anthologies *Alberta Rebound* (NeWest Press, 1990) and *Boundless Alberta* (NeWest Press, 1993). Her first book of fiction, *Mostly Country,* was published by NeWest Press in 1991 in their Nunatak new fiction series.

Nixon received her Bachelor of Education from The University of Calgary. She studied French for a year in Belgium and France and lived for two years in Zaire where she taught history and English as a second language. She presently writes in Calgary where she also teaches creative writing and freelances as a writing consultant.